"There [ ] to worry. I told you—"

Jeremy cut her off. "You told me the girl would have more sense. Now tell me, when did you plan all this?"

"But I—"

"My father left the decision making for the company with me," he said suddenly as if in answer to a question she'd asked. "And I have free rein. So if your friend believes she'll be a wealthy woman if she marries my brother, she's mistaken. They can't marry! Tell her that!"

Jeremy screeched the car to a stop. *This can't be happening,* Melissa told herself. But it was.

The closeness she had felt in his arms was like a dream. His kiss, his touch, his murmured words of endearment had seemed so beautiful. The only logical explanation was that Jeremy had been pretending.

Virginia Hart comes from a family of writers. Her sister writes mysteries, and her husband—who's even more romantic than Virginia's "heroes"—is an award-winning country music songwriter. Virginia, not to be outdone, has written mysteries, historical romances, Westerns, and now Harlequin Romances. Confusion is the order of the day at the Harts' Burbank, California, home, with Virginia at her typewriter, cola in hand—she says she's addicted—and her husband composing and singing at the top of his lungs. Their two sons, no doubt, add to the creative chaos.

Sweet Pretender

Virginia Hart

Harlequin Books

TORONTO • NEW YORK • LONDON
AMSTERDAM • PARIS • SYDNEY • HAMBURG
STOCKHOLM • ATHENS • TOKYO • MILAN

ISBN 0-373-02811-3

Harlequin Romance first edition January 1987

CHAPTER ONE

MELISSA'S EYES SKIMMED THE TEAROOM in Hammond's Department Store before being drawn to the hallway in front of the employees' elevators. Her younger sister Arlene, still in her apron, was gesturing madly to attract her attention.

"Now what is so important it can't wait until tonight?" Melissa asked with a touch of impatience. "There's a meeting in my boss's office and I can't afford to be late back from my coffee break. I'm not exactly Mr. Lowell's idea of a department head anyway."

Arlene wasn't listening. She was peering into the tearoom, where everything was pleasantly serene. Greenery cascaded profusely from macramé and beadwork planters set into the ceiling, and vines twined in and out of the lattice-covered walls, accentuating the outdoorsy feeling and the refreshing coolness made possible by an excellent air-conditioning system. A gentle fall of water tinkled from a fish-shaped fountain, and chartreuse parakeets in white cages cooperatively raised their voices to provide entertainment for the diners. But Arlene, who worked in Albany's most popular tearoom, seemed immune to its relaxing environment and the haven it provided for weary afternoon shoppers. She was intent on seeing something else.

"Look," she said at last. "There she is."

"There who is?" Melissa's eyes followed her sister's pointing finger to a table by the window. An attractive woman in her mid-thirties sat alone, picking at a dinner salad as if fearful of what she might find under a lettuce leaf.

"Mrs. Kerr. Who else?"

"I can't believe you brought me all the way over here for this."

"Isn't she beautiful?"

"I don't care what she looks like." Melissa jabbed the elevator's Down button. "I don't approve of her or her offer to employ you. Mother and Dad wouldn't, either."

"It isn't exactly employment," Arlene persisted. "It's more like an offer of an exciting all-expenses-paid holiday. With a salary besides. Think about it. If I'd won this chance on a TV show, you'd be shouting 'hooray.' "

"You didn't win it. Besides, we've already made arrangements for our vacation. In Boston."

"Boston! I've already seen the Bunker Hill Monument and Old Ironsides."

"There's more to Boston than that. Our grandmother for instance."

"We can drive over and see her any weekend of the year. I think two days is all she can take of us, anyhow."

"Us?" Melissa raised an eyebrow. "You're the one who wears her out. Besides, why should this Kerr woman want to hire you to impersonate her daughter? The more I think about it, the more unsavory it sounds."

"Unsavory." Arlene wrinkled her nose. "You make her sound like a bowl of stew."

"A stew is exactly what you'd be in half the time, if I agreed to your escapades." A bell rang, the Down light blinked on, and the elevator doors slid open. "Aren't you supposed to be working?"

"I've got a split shift today, remember?"

"Then scoot along home and don't forget to pick up some coffee at the market. We're all out, and I won't have time."

"Coffee!" Arlene groaned.

"Yes, coffee. You're the one who can barely stumble to the table in the morning without it." Melissa glanced at her watch and shook her head. "Of all the times for me to be late. Mr. Lowell plans to discuss the best way to discourage tardiness in employees."

As they stepped off the elevator on the ground floor, Arlene touched a hand to her sister's shoulder. "Don't walk so fast, Missy. I have to explain something—make you understand how different we are. Take your eyes for example."

"What do my eyes have to do with it?"

"They're the same sparkling green as our Scottish grandmother's. You're petite like Gram, too. And you stay that way, lucky you, without ever having to resort to dry toast and non-fat milk."

"There's some point to this inventory, I take it?"

"I, on the other hand, have eyes that are a heavenly blue, like the eyes of our forever-handsome and dashing papa. I'm taller than you by nearly three inches, and my figure is too curvy to be classified as petite. But, I might add, those curves are all in the right places."

"You forgot to mention that you're a modest little thing as well."

"I'm satisfied with my appearance," Arlene countered. "Why shouldn't I be? I'm stuck with it."

"Why indeed? Now will you disappear and let me get on with my day? Or do you want to see me fired?"

"Won't you listen? It's important. You can draw and paint like..."

"Like Rembrandt?"

"Better than that, if you ask me. I can't draw a straight line, even with a ruler. But I'm a wicked pianist, while you struggle over 'Chopsticks.'"

Melissa exhaled through clenched teeth. "I'm giving you one final warning before I—"

"What I'm trying to say, dear, is that I'm an adult now. Capable of making my own decisions. We're different people, you and I. Not only in our appearance, but in the way we feel inside. What you like, I might abhor, and vice versa. What would be wrong for you—"

"Is wrong for you, too." The revolving door slowed maddeningly as Arlene, giggling, squeezed into the same section Melissa had chosen. Fortunately the insurance company where Melissa worked was only half a block away. If she hurried she could still make the meeting before everyone had settled in the conference room. "We'll discuss this later," she promised when they were outside.

"There's nothing to discuss. Oh, listen, I'd be an ungrateful wretch if I didn't appreciate all you've done for me. If you hadn't agreed to play mother to me four years ago, I'd have had to go with our folks when Dad took that horrible job in Saudi Arabia. Just imagine me living in a place where a woman has to be escorted everywhere. I couldn't jog or ride horseback or even play tennis. I couldn't go to the market without a man to guard me. I want to please you, Melissa. Truly I do. But this time..."

"This time?"

Arlene stopped walking. "I've already told Mrs. Kerr I accept her offer. I'll be able to earn in a single summer what it would have taken me the whole year to squirrel away. We'll be able to take our trip to the Greek islands much earlier than we'd planned. You already have your part saved."

"You'd have yours, too, if you hadn't bought that wickedly expensive stereo equipment."

"If, if, if. If we had wings we could fly to Greece under our own power and save air fare. See you later." Arlene wiggled her fingers and began to back away.

"Count on it," Melissa called after her as she hurried back to work.

All heads turned as she slid into the meeting room. Mr. Lowell stopped speaking, cleared his throat and scowled as she took one of the small notebooks and sharpened pencils that had been provided and found a seat.

"Miss Brandon, we are discussing the horrendous number of employee-hours lost," Mr. Lowell told her with raised eyebrows, "by workers taking too long over coffee breaks. By their too-frequent visits to the drinking fountains and to the lavatories."

Melissa nodded and held her pencil poised.

"I like to remember what Longfellow once said." Mr. Lowell picked up the sign that sat on the desk before him and read with all the emotion Sir Laurence Olivier would have invested in Hamlet's soliloquy:

"The heights of great men reached and kept
Were not attained by sudden flight
But they, while their companions slept
Were toiling upward, through the night."

The meeting progressed slowly. Someone from the Claims Department suggested that a merit and demerit system be devised for punishing the guilty and rewarding the virtuous. Two underwriters from Inland Marine, who were seated behind Melissa, snickered through it all and whispered ridiculous suggestions for rewards: pretty file clerks sacrificing themselves semi-annually to those who accumulated merits; a camel-of-the-Month scroll to be presented to the employee who stayed away from the drinking fountain for the longest period of time; chamber pots under all the desks to save trips to the rest rooms.

Melissa hardly heard them. She could think only of Arlene and this new trouble the girl was planning to make for herself. By the time five o'clock arrived she all but ran out the door, her mind bursting with things she wanted to say when she got home.

"Miss Brandon," someone called.

"Yes?"

She was certain she would have remembered if she'd seen the young man before. He was tall, with sun-streaked dark blond hair and an engaging smile. "Natalie Kerr wanted me to have a word with you."

Aha! That was it. After their conversation Arlene had made a beeline to Mrs. Kerr and told the woman that Melissa objected to her dubious offer of employment. "If you don't mind," she told him crisply, "I'd rather say what has to be said on the way to the parking lot. It's been a long day."

"Fine with me."

His tan sport coat was an expensive one, she noted, and had probably been specially made to accommodate his shoulders, which were extremely broad in comparison with the leanness of the rest of him. His brown eyes were warm and his face—well—it would have been the perfect face for a man who hoped to talk someone into something.

"I'm Brian Hendricks," he said as they left the building. He offered his hand, along with the smile that had certainly toppled stronger resistances than hers. He hunched his shoulders and squinted at the sky. "I don't know about you, but I enjoy the feel of the sun when I'm doing any number of things in the great outdoors. But when I'm locked into a coat and tie and trying to impress a pretty girl with my charm, I can appreciate a summer day far better if I'm viewing it through a window, from somewhere that's air-conditioned."

Melissa sighed. The air was ovenlike. Besides, if she flew away without confronting Mr. Hendricks, he would flatter himself that she'd been intimidated by him.

"I suppose we could stop for a few minutes at the coffee shop and get this settled."

"Any oasis will do."

"Why didn't Mrs. Kerr come herself?" she asked when they'd settled into a booth and ordered coffee.

"She had an urgent appointment. But I can explain everything you might want to know about her plans."

I'll just bet you can, Melissa thought. *And you believe you can sweet-talk me into agreement.*

"You have an unusual sister," he went on. "Unusual in that she'd seek your approval. She is, after all, nineteen, isn't she?"

"Nineteen or ninety-five, she's still my sister."

"I understand. Natalie—Mrs. Kerr—is my sister, too, you see. There's nothing sinister about what she wants to do. Her problem is simple. She has an excess of pride."

"I don't understand."

"We were born, she and I, in Sandgate, a village in Connecticut. It's—"

"I know where it is," she assured him, hoping to cut short the story of his life by a few minutes.

He smiled tolerantly at the interruption. "I don't intend to bore you with a long family saga. But bear with me. Sandgate, being what it is, makes Natalie's problem what it is. Even more than in most small towns, everyone in Sandgate knows what everyone else is doing there. Lives merge, you might say."

"And what has that to do with Arlene?"

"When I was six, my parents decided they couldn't live under the same roof any longer. They couldn't, of course, remain in Sandgate and endure the gossip a divorce would cause, especially since we were only walking a tightrope at the edge of social acceptance anyway. My father had to work for a living. He was a salesman, and that put two strikes against us to start. So we moved to Albany."

Melissa looked at her watch. "I don't mean to be rude, but..."

"A moment longer, please. Natalie is older than I am, and at the time of our pulling up roots had just suffered the loss of her fiancé. Actually she was jilted in the cruelest sort of way. The man decided to marry someone more suited to his position in society."

"I still don't—"

"To keep up appearances, and not wanting her friends to pity her, she wrote all sorts of letters describing her new and exciting life in the big city. She wrote of her engagement and eventual marriage to a dashing, well-to-do older man who worshipped her, bought her everything a girl could dream of having and took her around the world.

"Later she wrote of her lovely daughter, Jean, who could dance, sing and play the piano like an angel—that is, if angels can do those things."

"And there was no husband," Melissa offered, deciding to give him only the time it would take her to see the bottom of her coffee cup. "No daughter."

"Actually everything was fairly much as she'd described it."

"Then . . . ?"

"Nat discovered that her doting husband was lavishing attention on another woman as well. Two women, in fact. One in Syracuse and another in Boston. She could have borne up under the shock of losing him. But Jean, who'd been a shy, submissive little thing until she turned sixteen, suddenly decided her life was meaningless and empty, that Nat was responsible for everything that had gone wrong with it. She packed up and went to live with her father."

"Girls of that age often choose their fathers," Melissa told him. "After a while she'll see the truth and come home."

"Not in time."

"In time for what?" Melissa forgot temporarily the seconds that were ticking away. It was touching to think that a young man who probably had pressing problems of his own could care so much about those his sister faced.

As if he sensed the change in her attitude, Brian relaxed visibly. His slow smile was one he might have worn had they been old friends talking over pleasant memories they shared. She almost wished they were. She liked him.

"Sandgate is two hundred years old this month. There's to be a gala week-long bicentennial to end all celebrations," he said. "There'll be something slated for every night. Dances, dinner parties, you name it. Nat accepted all invitations with relish long before her breakup with her husband. She wanted to show off how well life had treated her. Now suddenly, there is no life...."

Melissa didn't interrupt him, though she could think of any number of solutions. A woman who had no qualms about hiring someone to stand in for her daughter shouldn't mind inventing an attack of yellow fever or, at least, of chicken pox.

Her thought processes must have shown in her face because Brian broke off in the middle of his explanation, smiled with a kind of sadness in his eyes and shrugged. "A husband's absence at such an earth-shaking occasion," he told her, "might be attributed to the acceptable chasing of the almighty dollar. There could be a meeting of corporate heads halfway across the world or trouble in an African diamond mine. But a daughter's absence as well? Suspicion would begin to unravel the threads of Natalie's tale. In her youth, she'd acquired a partly deserved reputation for stretching the truth anyway. She considers it an act of God that her feet gave out on a shopping spree the day she stopped into the tearoom and caught sight of Arlene."

"Arlene resembles your niece that closely?"

"She wouldn't fool anyone who's seen Jean in person, no. But the likeness is sharp enough to pull the trick on someone who's only seen photographs. She's graceful and beautiful. Everything Nat would want in a daughter. And as a bonus, she plays the piano."

"Yes, she's exceptionally talented."

"Then you'll send her on her mission of mercy with your blessing?"

Melissa traced the rim of her cup with one finger. "I didn't say that. I don't like the idea of my sister living a lie."

"Did Julie Andrews lie when she pretended to be Mary Poppins? Did Elizabeth Taylor lie when she masqueraded as Cleopatra?"

"You're confusing me, Mr. Hendricks."

"I hope so."

Melissa had never been one to make snap judgments. But somehow, she trusted him. It wasn't that he was nice looking. Jack the Ripper could well have been fair of face. No, perhaps it was the direct way he looked into her eyes. The lack of guile in his manner.

Their talk took much longer than she'd expected it would. By the time she arrived home and let herself in, she was running late. A tureen of steaming seafood chowder explained the delicious smell that met her at the door. A white tablecloth had replaced the plastic cover that served for most of their meals, and the good soup bowls had been set out along with the silver. Debussy was on the stereo turntable, set low enough—for a change—to allow conversation. Arlene wore a Cheshire cat grin.

"Did you meet Mr. Hendricks?"

"I did."

"Then I'm going on a holiday."

"You're only half right, my pet." Melissa sailed past Arlene to attack her favorite dish. "*We're* going on a holiday."

"By we, you mean..."

"I mean we. You and I. I insisted. If you have no objections."

Arlene slapped a hand to her forehead. "I think it's fantastic. There'll be all sorts of wonderful-looking men there. Who knows? You might meet someone."

"Someone?"

"You know what I mean. You haven't gone out much since Mom and Dad left. I know it's because you felt you had to stay home and watch over me."

"You're talking nonsense."

"Just the same, I feel responsible for the lack of excitement in your social life." Arlene's dimples deepened when she smiled. She closed her eyes and pressed her fingers to her temples as if she were a mystic trying to peer into the future. "I see a man in your life. He's tall, dark and very handsome."

Melissa laughed and took her place at the table. "Never mind. I'll settle for two out of three. I've already met someone tall and handsome."

"You mean Brian Hendricks? Aha! So he's the reason you decided to tag along." Arlene sat down, too, but made no move to ladle chowder into her bowl. "I thought as much."

"I'm going, my girl, to keep an eye on you."

"I believe you," Arlene crooned, nodding in a way that said she didn't believe her at all.

"I want to be there if you need me."

"Of course you do," the girl said, still nodding.

"It's my vacation too, you know. I have two weeks coming to me, and I've always adored the sea air and the sand. Besides, I can't turn up at our grandparents' house without you. They'd ask a million questions."

"I know."

"Don't you realize that it's..." Melissa began, but changed her mind. She wasn't going to convince her sister that Brian wasn't the reason she was going to Sandgate.

Well, let Arlene believe what she would. Melissa would be saved a lot of worry. Arlene wouldn't be alone in a village of hostile strangers if Natalie's plan hit a snag.

CHAPTER TWO

THE BOX-SHAPED HOUSE set on a gentle slope was white clapboard, with creaking steps that led up a curving path to the rickety porch. Inside, the walls were slate gray. The ceiling was gray as well, with rough-hewn beams, and the floor was scrubbed plank with rag rugs here and there to soften the barnlike effect.

Two marvelous small-paned windows on either side of the pegged door compensated for any gloom that might have pervaded the rest of the house. They began almost at the ceiling and were deepset, to accommodate window seats wide enough to allow a person to curl up and sleep comfortably—if that person was as travel-weary as Melissa was now.

The wall opposite the door was given to a massive stone fireplace. Ancient ladles, bed warmers and practical-looking implements of all descriptions hung before it, as if expecting someone to put them to use. In the center of the main room hung a twisted iron light fixture that held candles, and hurricane lamps sat on several of the chunky chests and side tables. Melissa couldn't help but wonder if the owner was a romantic who liked the effect of lamplight, or if the area was subject to heavy storms that caused power failure.

She had insisted on taking her own car, in case she and Arlene decided to head back to Albany before Natalie was ready to go. Natalie had insisted just as strongly that Arlene ride with her to give them time to get their stories straight. So two cars had been needed for the trip to Sandgate.

Since Melissa had drawn Brian as guide and map reader, and since he fancied himself an expert on that part of the country, their side trips had been numerous. They'd followed almost every highway sign that pointed the way to tourist sites, taken pictures of each other at historical markers, and Natalie and Arlene had arrived at their destination well before them.

Natalie had changed into an ankle-length silk kimono in a Chinese red that showed to advantage the slim, youthful line of her figure. Her hair was pulled into a cluster of golden curls at the nape of her neck. She was a stunning woman, but, except for her blond coloring and her deep brown eyes, she bore no resemblance to her brother. She was as proud and aware of her beauty as he was natural and unassuming.

"You look tired, dear," she said to Melissa. "I'll show you to your room."

My room? Melissa mused. Evidently she wouldn't be sharing a bedroom with her sister, after all. "Where's Arlene?" she asked as they started up the stairs.

Mrs. Kerr stopped with a hand on the banister and waited a dramatic moment before answering. "Miss Brandon—Melissa—I hope you don't think I'm being overly critical of you. We're pleased to have you here. But I must ask you to remember that in Sandgate your sister is not your sister, and her name is not Arlene. It's Jean."

"I didn't think it mattered when no one was around to hear."

"A slip of the tongue at the wrong time could ruin all my plans. It might be well to get used to the name."

"I'll remember." Mrs. Kerr was right, Melissa told herself. Still, she couldn't help but feel a bit James Bondish about the whole thing. "Where is she?"

Natalie nodded toward a door at the opposite end of the hall from the one she opened for Melissa. "Her room is adjoining mine. Yours is somewhat small, I'm sorry to say. But I believe you'll find it comfortable enough for a short stay."

Was there unusual emphasis on the word "short"? Or was she only touchy because she was tired?

"I'll be fine," she said.

"There won't be time for you to visit with Jean now. The wheels have already begun to turn. Tonight's banquet marks the opening of the bicentennial celebration, and reservations were made before we knew you were going to be with us. There's room only for three, I'm afraid."

"It's quite all right."

"There's tea in the cupboard, and there are tins of soup if you're hungry. There are biscuits in the breadbox and, of course, eggs in the fridge. You'll be alone for a time. I hope you don't find things too dull."

"Don't worry about me," Melissa told her, marveling that anyone could find such a place dull. The house was nothing special, but it was only a short walk to sand and sea. Anticipation of quiet time on the beach with damp sand between her bare toes and water lapping against her ankles lifted her spirits, and she decided against taking a nap.

"I'll fly then." Natalie paused at the landing. "Don't forget, should you meet anyone, anyone at all, don't tell them you have a sister. Don't tell them anything. Just say you're a friend of my brother's, come to join in the festivities."

Natalie hadn't exaggerated when she said Melissa's room was small. It was only a few paces across, and the sloping ceiling made it impossible to straighten up in a third of it. There was no closet. Only a mahogany wardrobe with a half mirror on the inside of one of its doors.

But she had her own window seat and a wide window that swung in to allow her to enjoy the cool sea breezes. A lingering warm bath would have been relaxing, but the day was passing, and she was determined to enjoy what was left of it.

By the time she'd showered, the house was quiet. Everyone had left. She was slightly miffed that her sister hadn't insisted on seeing her. But she brushed aside negative thoughts and slipped into a pair of jeans. After donning an oversized tailored shirt and a pair of canvas sneakers, she pinned up the glossy tumble of her long black hair to secure it against the wind and plopped on her white sailor hat with its brim turned down.

As she started on her way, she had to smile. Slim-hipped as she was and shiny-faced from her shower, she would have needed only a sand pail and shovel to complete the picture of a young boy combing the beach for shells and bits of driftwood.

Night hadn't closed in completely, but there were lighted windows in most of the houses along her way. The lowering fog made it seem later than it actually was.

The village had evidently sprung up with little thought given to street planning. Dwellings were built in a one-by-one haphazard way. She had to zig up one street and zag down another for some distance before she reached the seawall. It would have been more pleasant if Arlene could have accompanied her, but since it couldn't be so, it didn't matter. She had never been one to mourn moments of solitude.

Walking through the grayish mist, she had a sense of drifting out of time. There were few passersby and no sounds, other than the sounds of the water and an occasional blast from a distant foghorn. A curious melancholy swept over her as she noticed that many of the houses had been constructed with widow's walks atop them. Some were built simply as decorative features of the architecture. But others, especially in the older houses, looked as if they'd served a real purpose in time of storm and squall. She thought of the countless young wives and mothers who had stood on those walks, shivering against the cold—waiting, hoping, praying for their men to come home safe from the sea.

Melissa removed her shoes and stepped onto the sand. The going was smooth for a time, but when scattered stones gave way to boulders, the beach became a narrow strip. She could barely see the water now, but she could hear it. For long moments she stood listening, imagining she heard the sound a small boat might make, sliding through the dark water. A boat manned by buccaneers who planned to bury their stolen treasure deep in the sand, along with the unfortunates who did the digging.

She shivered, put her shoes on again and began to walk faster this time. She heard the youngsters, but didn't see them soon enough to keep from stumbling over their ice chest. She fell sprawling into their midst, and there was a wild scramble.

"Hey!"

"Watch it."

"I'm sorry," Melissa murmured, noticing that she had not only startled them but scattered a tower they'd built.

"It's okay," one boy told her. He was about thirteen, as were the others with him. He wore a nylon windbreaker and shorts. His feet were bare. "But you scared the bird off. We almost had him."

"What bird?"

Another of the boys pointed. They'd evidently been trying to surround a gray seabird, who, in spite of a badly drooping wing, was doing a good job of evading them.

"We have to go. We're late now, and one of us has to kill him first."

"Kill him?" Melissa was horrified. "Why?"

"He's hurt real bad," a towheaded girl said. "Even if his injuries don't get him, the other birds'll pick him to death. My dad says the kindest thing to do is—"

"No!" Melissa didn't want to hear. "Can't you take him home?"

"No way. We've got cats."

"Us too."

"We don't have any cats," the girl said. "But my mom'd skin me if I brought another hurt bird home. They always die anyhow, and my little brother bawls about it for days."

"Shh!" The boy in the windbreaker held a finger to his lips.

Everyone fell silent as the smallest of their number dropped to his knees and began to inch his way toward a rock where the quivering bird was attempting to secrete himself under a pile of seaweed. A hand shot out and there was a cry of triumph.

"Got him!"

"Don't hurt him," Melissa pleaded.

"You take him, then."

"I can't."

"She could take him to Eli."

"Who's Eli?"

"Eli Campbell. Some weirdo who knows all about birds. He lives in a shack up there. Through those trees." The girl blew her hair out of her eyes and pointed to rickety steps that led up and away from the beach. "The path leads straight to his door."

Melissa drew back. "Couldn't you and your friends..."

"Nope. We're gonna catch it now. We were supposed to head back an hour ago."

"But..."

"Eli won't hurt you," the girl said. "He's just strange. He's not a criminal or anything."

"It's because he drinks," the boy in the windbreaker added, struggling with his towel, a blanket and a canvas bag of canned soft drinks. "He used to be a doctor, they say. A people doctor. His wife died, and he didn't want to practice medicine anymore. Mom says he's trying to make Sandgate dry by drinking up all the whiskey in the village."

"If anybody can save the bird, it's Eli Campbell. Loads of people bring hurt things to him. He even has a cage on his porch in case folks come round when he's gone."

"We always leave something on his table to pay him," the girl said. "Don't hand him money, though. Father says it might hurt his pride."

"If you don't want to take him to Eli," the smallest boy offered, "I can kill him real quick. He won't suffer and—"

"No!" Melissa reached for the still-struggling bird. "Give him to me."

She had to walk carefully. The steps were splintery, her vision was limited in the fog and growing darkness, and there was no handhold. If she were to lose her balance, she might hurt the poor little guy worse than he was hurt already.

"There, there," she whispered, wondering at the birds rapid heartbeat. "You're so pretty. And you're strong. You'll be fine. Eli will know what to do."

Eli's cottage sat on blocks. It was weatherbeaten and grayed, and its plain plank door was hollowed out at the handle from many openings and closings. Along the side of the house was a tar paper shelter, well-stacked with firewood and housing what might have been Robinson Crusoe's raft, fashioned from tree limbs lashed together. There were fishing nets and barrels, broken kegs and crates, hooks and rolls of twine. An anchor had been fastened to one of the four-by-four supports along with a part of an old ship with the name *Lenore* painted in neat black letters.

The porch wasn't a porch at all, but rather a series of steps made from split logs. There was so much clutter that at first she didn't notice the cages the children had mentioned. A small one sat to the side of the stoop, and a large, walk-in one had been constructed on the other.

She raised the hinged cover on the smallest cage and allowed her prisoner to flutter free. He snuggled deep into the dried grass and uttered a halfhearted squawk. "I'll get the doctor."

When her third knock on the door brought no answer, Melissa moved around to the window, where an inch of yellow light shone between the sill and the shade. She'd no sooner bent down to look inside, than she felt herself being hoisted off her feet.

"Damn you!" a man shouted at her. "Didn't you do enough damage on your last visit?"

"Wait! Please!" she protested, abandoning her struggle quickly when she realized that his iron grip would still be fastened on her shirt if she managed to wriggle free. "You must have me mixed up with someone else."

"I suppose you're here selling magazine subscriptions."

"Let me go and I'll—"

"I'll let you go. I ought to whale you good. But I think I'll wait and let your father do it." As he dragged her into the cottage, Melissa lost one of her shoes, bumped her head on a support post and whacked an elbow on a door frame. Her outcries didn't stop him, though. He pushed her through the door, still berating her, and hurled her into a heap on the floor.

His back was to her now. He was searching through the incredible clutter on the desk. Could she—dare she—try to make an escape now? What an idiot she'd been to come here.

"He's a weirdo, but he isn't dangerous," one of the children had assured her. And she had accepted that assurance. What had possessed her?

When he faced her again, he was holding a torn square of paper and a ballpoint pen. "I want your name and your telephone number."

His appearance took her aback—and then some. She'd visualized Eli Campbell as a smallish man of about sixty-five, with stooped shoulders and a red-veined bulbous nose. The man who towered above her was none of these things. He was a man who would have warranted a second look and probably a good, long third if she'd met him under ordinary circumstances. His features were strong looking but well made and striking. He was at least as tall as Brian. The rolled-up sleeves of his denim shirt showed thickly muscled forearms, and there was only a scattering of gray in his black, Gypsylike hair. The expression on his face wasn't one of grief, but of anger. No. Anger was too mild a word. It was rage, and it was directed at her.

"I came with an injured bird. I believe its wing is broken. Some children told me—"

"And where is this bird?" he snarled. "Under your hat?"

His sarcasm tweaked her pride, enabling her to swallow her fear and answer with indignant deliberation. "I put it in the holding cage outside. Isn't that customary?"

"It's customary, yes." With a jerking movement, he turned up the lamp. His eyes made a quick but thorough sweep of her, eyebrows to ankles and back, accusing her without words of wearing a deliberate disguise. "You aren't one of them."

"No, I'm not. Whoever they might be."

"I'm sorry about this," he said, not sounding terribly sorry. "There's been trouble with vandals this past couple of weeks. Kids with too much time on their hands. I've been waiting for the chance to catch one of them in action."

"And you caught me instead."

"So it seems. Their ringleader is a boy about your size, who wears the same sort of..." He fluttered a hand toward Melissa's sailor hat. "Last night he smashed one of the windows in the shed and made off with some tools."

"And you thought I was that boy."

"It was a natural mistake."

"Natural?" she snapped. "Because I'm short."

"Not at all. If it hadn't been for the dim light and the fog, I couldn't possibly have missed the fact that you're a woman." Again his eyes took their inventory, this time more slowly.

"You might have taken a moment to be sure I was one of your culprits, before you pounced on me," she said, ignoring his silent approval.

"I might have. But, then, you might have gotten away. What were you doing on the beach anyway?"

"Walking."

"Do you have a beach card?"

She refused his offer of a hand up and rose under her own power. Her head still hurt from the whack she'd received, and she couldn't locate her left shoe. "Why should I need a beach card?"

"It's a private beach."

She remembered then. Her shoe was still outside, caught between the steps. Brushing past him without ceremony, she retrieved it, wriggled into it and came back inside to study herself briefly in the small, half-silvered excuse for a mirror that hung on a nail next to the door. She did look like something of an urchin. Wisps of dark hair had escaped her hat, and there was grime on her face. From the look of her dirty sneakers, they would never be white again.

"The idea of a beach being private appalls me," she snapped, turning on him. "No one should be allowed to own the rocks, sand and water, any more than they can own the sunshine. The beauties of nature are for everyone to enjoy."

"A very pretty speech, but perhaps you wouldn't feel that way if you could see the remnants of sandwiches, empty beer cans and broken bottles I find after a family of your nature lovers has gone."

"And Sandgate people never leave trash behind?"

"If they do, they soon hear about it. Besides, it's an easy matter to get a beach card. A visitor can stop in the sheriff's office and—"

"I've brought an injured bird," she broke in, trying to recover from chagrin at her disheveled appearance with a show of arrogance to match that of her host. This man was not your everyday brand of hermit. He showed no timidity at her intrusion. No fear of the outside world.

On the contrary, he was the personification of self-confidence. He gave the impression of being handsome, though the raw angles of his face kept him from being classically so. The line between his heavy straight brows said clearly that he was more given to frowning than smiling. But there was a glimmer in his deepset eyes. A glimmer that remained even when his expression was stern, hinting at some inner joke—a joke at her expense.

"So you said."

"If you're going to see to him, I think you should do it."

The frown line deepened. "There's coffee on the stove," he told her. "Help yourself. I'll see what I can do."

The coffee was bitter and so strong it made her eyes water. It wasn't even hot, but she sipped it for want of something to do, while the man brought the bird inside and worked over it. At first glance she had pronounced the cottage a disaster area. A hopeless shambles. Now that she'd studied it more closely, she realized that it only appeared so because it was overcrowded with possessions.

The doctor was a collector, it seemed. Of everything. Old clocks, maps, lithographs, keys, books and a multitude of things that defied category. There wasn't a bare spot on any wall or a clear place on any flat surface, except for the kitchen table. The floor was well swept, though. The curtains were clean, and there were no dirty dishes soaking in the sink.

"It isn't too bad. He's a sea swallow." The man held the patient up for her inspection. "I've taped his wing. He should be as good as new in a few days."

"What could have caused such an injury?"

"A stone, I'd guess."

"You mean someone deliberately hurt him?"

"It's been known to happen."

"It's hard to imagine." Disconcerted by her host's unrelenting gaze, she forced her eyes away. "He's beautiful, isn't he?"

The bird's underbody was soft shades of gray. His beak was scarlet, and he had a black velvety cap. He was relaxed now, sensing that he was among friends.

"If you think he's beautiful now, you should see him in flight."

"I hope I will." Did it sound as if she were inviting herself back?

He opened a curtained-off area at the far end of the room, where two layers of cages were secured to long shelves. Most were occupied. A larger cage, somewhat apart from the others, held another bird, exactly like the one she had rescued.

"I'll set yours in with her. A bird responds best to treatment if there's another of his kind about." Gently he eased the newcomer in and waited before fastening the door. "I'll have to watch to see how they get along," he said, yanking the curtain closed. "Sometimes an old-timer will resent a stranger for no apparent reason."

"They're much like people then," she couldn't resist saying.

Only the slightest trace of a smile indicated that the remark had struck home. She could have counted to ten slowly before he answered. "You might say that."

Fortunately she had tucked a few dollars into her jeans pocket, thinking to stop somewhere for a sandwich if she got hungry. Now she recalled what the children had said, and as the doctor turned to wash his hands at the sink, she put the money on the table and weighted it with a pepper shaker. It somehow made her feel foolish.

His back was turned, but he was studying her in the mirror. "Have you had your supper?"

She smiled. He was still treating her as he might have treated a child he had scolded for being naughty. Now he was being solicitous to make up for it. "I'm not hungry."

"I think you are. The sea air builds up an enormous appetite. We'll have something to eat. Then I'll see you home."

"It isn't necessary. Really." His food supplies, judging by the cupboard space and the tiny refrigerator, must have been limited. She didn't want him to feel that he had to entertain her.

"I didn't suppose it was necessary. I'd like to get to know you better."

His remark and the unexpected intensity of its delivery jarred her more than a little. Oh, she'd heard the same words from other men before. She'd seen the same look of interest in other men's eyes when she'd met them. But this man wasn't an ordinary man. He was the village hermit. Hermits didn't seek companionship from anyone, especially not from a stranger. Did they?

"You want to see if I'm worthy?" she countered.

He partly closed one eye. "Worthy?"

"Worthy of having a beach card." As always, when she felt ill at ease in someone's presence, she found herself joking. Though in this case, she was half in earnest. It still seemed wrong—no matter the reason—that any one group of people should have the right to grant or deny others permission to enjoy the gifts of nature.

"Something like that." He dried his hands and turned to face her. "Shall we go?"

Watch it, girl, she cautioned herself. *When you supposed this man was dangerous, you could have been right.* Dangerous in a different way. She knew nothing about him, except that he was the town eccentric.

"You're not planning to eat here?"

"My own cooking?" He shook his head as if dismissing an abhorrent thought. "Put that in the jam jar on the shelf over by the stove." He indicated the money she'd left on the table. "Eli will find it later."

"You—you aren't Eli Campbell?"

"You thought that?" Amusement twinkled in his eyes. "Sometimes I wish I was. He has a simple, uncomplicated life here. At least he had until recently. The vandals I mentioned threw rocks at the house. He bolted after them, took a tumble and twisted his leg. Now he's in the hospital. But he'll be out tomorrow. I've been seeing to things for him. My name is Jeremy York."

"Oh," was all she could say. It certainly made more sense that this man wasn't the recluse she'd expected.

However it was even more disturbing. Now he was a total stranger.

"And you are . . ." He waited.

"Melissa Brandon."

"Well, Melissa Brandon, how about it? The Sea View restaurant is only a short walk up the path to the road."

"I don't know."

"Sandgate people are honorable and above suspicion," he assured her, sensing the reason for her reluctance.

"Then the vandals you spoke of were summer people?"

"Without a doubt."

"How could I have thought otherwise?"

She'd never found it difficult to decline an unwelcome invitation before, she reminded herself. Or to shy away from an uncertain relationship. The key phrases here were no, thank you and goodbye uttered in a firm, emphatic voice. But she didn't say anything, and he moved closer.

For a moment she thought he was going to kiss her. Instead of stepping back, she tensed for it. She wanted it in a way—yet she didn't.

"You have a lovely face," he said. "But I'm certain you already know that."

"Thank you," she murmured. *You aren't so bad yourself,* she added silently.

"What you may not know is that your face is almost as dirty as it is lovely." He gestured with one hand. "The bathroom is in there. Why don't you do something about yourself? Your hair. That wretched hat. I'll see how our feathered friends are getting on together and we'll be on our way."

As she shut herself into the dollhouse-sized bathroom, she felt as jittery and weak-kneed as she had on the night of her first school dance.

You could be making a gigantic mistake, she warned her bedraggled reflection. If Arlene were in her place, Melissa would demand that she make for the door. She'd never known anyone quite like this man, terrific-looking and unpredictable. And the fact that she was inordinately attracted to him wasn't a plus; it could cloud her judgment. Could? It already had. And she wasn't that experienced.

The men in her life up to now had been those she'd known from the insurance company or from high school, and they'd been as predictable as television commercials.

She sighed, recognizing the futility of her argument. Maybe she'd regret getting involved with Jeremy York. But then going out for a sandwich was hardly "getting involved." And one thing was certain: should she let him get away without trying to learn something about him, she'd regret that, too.

CHAPTER THREE

AS THE NAME SUGGESTED, the redeeming quality of the Sea View restaurant was the magnificent view it no doubt afforded of the water. Wrapped in fog now, it was only a harshly lit diner, with chrome-and-vinyl booths and a frazzled young waitress who looked as if she had put in a long day and was ready to go home. There was only one other customer. A bearded man who worked a newspaper crossword. He didn't look up as Melissa and her companion entered.

Famished, Melissa ordered bacon and eggs. The man who sat opposite her seconded her decision without glancing at the menu. His deepset eyes were curious beneath eyebrows that were dark, shaggy gashes.

"What do you do, young lady," he asked, "when you aren't prowling about private beaches, peering into strange windows?"

"I'm an insurance underwriter in Albany," she said, then added quickly, "It might sound like dull work, but it isn't. I find it very challenging. A bit more study and I'll have my broker's license."

Restrained humor played at one corner of his mouth, lifting it slightly. "Why so defensive?"

"Am I?"

"Aren't you?"

She pulled her gaze to her water glass, suddenly finding the intense gray of his eyes—open and changing like the sky before a storm—too disquieting for direct contact. "Maybe."

She'd almost forgotten herself and explained that her younger sister, who had her own sights set on a glamorous musical career, couldn't imagine how Melissa could even consider such a dull, plodding occupation that meant staring at columns of figures all day. The mention of a sister could bring up questions she'd been advised not to answer. In Sandgate, as Natalie had reminded her, she had no sister.

"And what do you do," she mimicked him, finding her sense of direction again, "when you aren't frightening the living daylights out of trespassers?"

"I wouldn't have guessed that you could be frightened so easily."

"Easily? I thought I'd been set upon by a wild man."

"And so you had. Poor little girl." He gave her the half smile again. The one that worked only one side of his generously molded mouth. "But I was easily tamed, wasn't I?"

Tamed? She wondered. Even as he spoke—his voice as quietly resonant as that of a television newscaster and his manner gentle—there was something of the wild man she had encountered in Eli's shack about him still, boiling and bubbling beneath the surface. The idea of this duality intrigued her.

"What do you do?" she repeated, genuinely interested. Perhaps if she brought the level of their conversation to the everyday mechanics of going to and from work, to briefcases, account books and computers, she'd see him as an ordinary person and recognize her overreaction to him.

"I build amusement park equipment."

"Carousels . . . and Ferris wheels?"

"Among other things."

Impossible. She frowned, considering him. Never would she have imagined him in such a line of work. The Tarzanlike thickness of his neck and shoulders and the obvious strength of his form would certainly have been compatible with one who worked by the sweat of his brow, felling trees, climbing mountains and battling forest fires. But there was a dignity and noble grace about him, too, that said something else. Even in his faded denims he had the look of a handsome young ambassador taking a well-deserved leave from the pressing duties of his office.

"Most people have the idea that spectacular theme rides are new," he said. "They aren't. The Exposition of Buffalo, New York, in 1901, for example, had a Trip to the Moon ride so realistic that when passengers emerged, they couldn't believe they hadn't actually left the ground. Then there was the Fall of Pompeii attraction that reenacted the eruption of Mount Vesuvius."

Melissa groaned. "That's entertainment? You don't make anything so grisly, do you?"

"I prefer rides that make the customer a participant, rather than an observer. We're working on one now that's a much-improved version of the old Steeplechase. The horses run on separate tracks, and riders have the sensation of jockeying in an actual horse race."

Clearly he loved his work. As he described this or that attraction, giving dates and places and relating anecdotes that made her laugh, growing enthusiasm cast him in a new role. Again she adjusted the mental image she was forming of him, adding youthful exuberance and passion for life's challenges.

His was a contagious passion, too, enabling Melissa to follow with interest as he outlined in detail a problem he'd run across in a newly conceived ride's design. He was an exciting man whose sensuality was present in his every word and movement. Had he been a plumber, he could probably have made her feel enthusiastic about an idea for a new kind of plunger.

"I haven't been to an amusement park since I was a child," she said, almost adding that it was because Arlene got dizzy on anything that spun, whirled or dipped.

"And now you're too adult. What a pity." His grave frown was a comic-opera one, born of a fondness for teasing, she suspected. "To waste your young years playing the sophisticate. Then when you're as old as I am, you'll try desperately to recapture the youth you allowed to slip away."

She slid her tongue lightly across her upper lip, wondering if a bit of bacon or a crumb of toast could be stuck there, warranting his close scrutiny. "I believe there's a moral in that," she said.

He leaned closer. "Ah, you noticed."

"I'm not exactly wasting my years," she answered guardedly. "And you aren't exactly an old man." Had he, after all, brought her out as he might have a child with a scraped knee for an ice-cream cone? Had she misjudged his interest in her? The thought was disheartening. Could she feel such a stirring without his feeling it, too?

She would have placed him at about thirty-five, if she were forced to hazard a guess. In any case, he was no more than ten years her senior. Undoubtedly he had misjudged her age, as many people did, because of her slight build.

He made no comment on her answer, nor did he react as if he'd heard it. But the silence that fell between them as he mulled something over in his mind was a comfortable one—the sort old friends might share who felt no need to make small talk. "Why Sandgate?" he asked abruptly, beckoning for the waitress to bring him a coffee refill.

The question caught her off guard. "Why not? The reunion festivities should be exciting."

He laughed explosively. "They'll be a crashing bore to anyone who isn't a native."

Melissa fought an impulse to pound a fist on the table. A native! There he was again, stressing the fact that she was an outsider. Brian had certainly been right about the clannishness of the townspeople. "I'm here with a friend," she said.

"I see."

The tentative half smile played at the corners of his mouth again as he waited for her to elaborate. She didn't. This time she didn't find his smile nearly so attractive nor the silence so comfortable. Too much resentment was building up inside her. A snob in any guise was still a snob.

"Do I need a permit to attend?" she asked, with more than a touch of saccharine. "And is it your duty to see that I have one?"

The smile fell away. "Are you always so touchy, or is there something about me that brings it out in you?" Clearly he would have said more if he had known her better. He wasn't used to being questioned.

"Do you always interrogate visitors to your fair community, or is there something about me that brings it out in you?" she countered.

His shaggy eyebrows pulled closer together. "I'm not the constable."

"You could have fooled me."

"I'm sorry if I sounded inhospitable," he said, tapping an impatient finger against the rim of his cup. He looked toward the door, probably anxious now to be rid of her. "The fog's getting thick out there. Finish up like a good girl and I'll see you home."

Like a good girl. She considered saying, "Thanks, but no thanks." She'd find her own way. But it would have been a foolhardy gesture. She might wander about for hours. The landmarks she'd chosen to lead her back might have been swallowed by the fog, just as the bread crumbs of Hansel and Gretel had been eaten by the birds of the forest. Besides, this man interested her, his attempts to bait her notwithstanding. She wasn't ready to walk away from him so soon. He was a puzzle she might well enjoy trying to solve.

"I've finished," she told him, primly touching the paper napkin to her lips.

A sense of mystery surrounded them as they moved away from the Sea View's neon lights. Was it only the mist, the call of the sea and the unfamiliar surroundings? Or was it the presence of the stranger who walked beside her? He was still a stranger, after all, though less so now that she knew his name. Jeremy York. She'd seen him scribble it on the check the waitress had brought to him. His was a dark, bold signature, with well-rounded letters and outsized capitals. If she'd known anything about graphology, she might have discovered something about him from it. Jeremy. She'd never known anyone by that name before. It had a feeling about it of another time and place—of dashing men in skintight breeches, who fought with swords to defend a lady's honor.

The road appeared to have no edges. It was like a fairy-tale setting from *Brigadoon* emerging only once every hundred years. Were they to stray too far either right or left, they might tumble on and on into eternity. A sleek black dog of indeterminate pedigree trotted out of nowhere. After sniffing their heels, it fell in behind them.

"Is he yours?" Melissa asked, noticing Jeremy's casual acceptance of the animal's presence.

"Yes and no. He's the village watchdog, you might say."

"Oh?"

"Trained from birth to rip limb from limb anyone who dares to venture into Sandgate without permission of the town council."

"Mmm." A surreptitious glance at his profile told her that while he was joking, he was still miffed. "Am I in danger?" she asked, feigning fear.

"Not if you stay close to me." He snaked a possessive arm around her slender middle and pulled her against him. "Closer. That's it. Let him believe we're friends."

The innocence of the dog's expression and its wagging tail belied Jeremy's threatening words, and she couldn't resist one small giggle. "I'm sorry," she said, not missing the stress he'd placed on the word "believe." "You were right. I have been touchy. I suppose it's because I'm tired. It's been a pleasant day, but a long one."

Though it was the best excuse she could offer, she wasn't really tired. She could have walked on and on without feeling a need to rest. For some indefinable reason she had dipped into a new storehouse of energy.

Jeremy stopped walking so abruptly that she was jolted off balance. He caught her to set her right, and the firm pressure of his fingers, warm, alien yet familiar, on her bare arm, sent a tremor through her that crimped her toes and all but set her teeth to chattering.

Would he consider her stumbling to be an often-used attempt at flirtation? Certainly he was a man used to the wiles of women, unless the women of Sandgate didn't recognize a good thing when they saw it. However, when with difficulty she forced her eyes to his, she knew he wasn't judging her. The bottomless depth of his gaze erased all notions she may have harbored that he thought of her as a child. Never had she felt so desirable. Never had she felt so strongly that she was about to be kissed.

Should she allow it? Would she have a choice? Her lips tingled deliciously in anticipation. He seemed already to be tasting them.

"We've made our peace then?" he asked.

She nodded, not trusting her voice.

"Good. Then I'd like to see to your education."

She swallowed hard. "To my what?"

"Don't scowl like that." His laugh was deep and genuine as he touched a finger to the place between her eyebrows where a frown might begin, making it the center of all her sensation. His teeth were squarish and very white in contrast to his deeply tanned skin. He must have spent many hours in the sun. She could visualize him now, climbing about on the gigantic frame of one of his daredevil rides. "I only meant I want to teach you how much fun there can be in the childlike pleasures."

"Such as?"

"I have some business in Westerly tomorrow. There's a fair nearby, and I'd like to spirit you away with me, if your friend won't object."

"No. That is—I'm not sure." Melissa wondered if she dared to say yes without checking first with Arlene.

"As I recall," he went on, "there's nothing earth-shaking on schedule for tomorrow afternoon. And I promise to have you back in time for the dance in the evening. You are planning to attend, I suppose."

A few persuasive words were all she needed. The prospect of going anywhere with Jeremy—to a carnival or to a mud-wrestling match—made her want to shout her acceptance.

"I don't see why I wouldn't be able to go to the fair," she managed, sounding as offhand as she could. Mentally she was going through her wardrobe, deciding what she could wear that would appear casual and still knock him off his feet.

"Good. There's just one thing I have to know before we go any farther."

A flux of vague possibilities passed through Melissa's mind, drawing her out of her reverie. She tried to sound unruffled. "What's that?"

"Are we headed in the right direction? Do you know where you're staying?"

"Oh—yes," she answered, relieved. For a moment she'd feared he would ask about her friend, and she hadn't yet decided what she should say. The mention of Brian could definitely throw cold water on their relationship at this embryonic stage. Without being told the entire story, Jeremy would never understand why she had chosen to attend the reunion with a man she knew only casually. And she didn't want to—she couldn't—resort to more lies. The ones imposed on her already by the masquerade would be hard enough to explain away if the need ever came.

"Would you like to give me a hint?" he teased, puzzling at her hesitation.

"Oh, of course. Let me see. We passed the War Memorial," she said slowly. "Checkpoint one. And the public library."

"Checkpoint two. Right."

"Now." Mentally she reversed the route she had taken through town. "We follow the stone steps up to the next street. Hilldale?"

"Hillcrest. Right." His arm went around her to steady her as they climbed and remained when she no longer needed steadying. Or did she?

She felt as if a song inside her were ready to burst free, as it happened in so many old movie musicals. *What's happening to me?* she wondered. She turned down dates sometimes—often—simply because she didn't like to leave Arlene alone. Or because she felt as if she'd prefer a quiet evening at home. Yet here she was, dragged into a ridiculous two weeks of role playing, partly because of an attraction for one man. *And now I'm hoping for the kisses of another.*

And you came along to watch after me? Arlene would squeal.

"In another minute we'll be running out of street," Jeremy cautioned her, his hand moving up her back in a tentative caress.

"At the corner we jog left, climb the hill and pass a yard with a stone menagerie. Ducks, rabbits, deer."

"Mrs. Blaker loves animals," he said dryly. "But only those that don't bark, eat or have to be exercised."

"Stonehurst Street should come in here soon." Melissa was less sure of her bearings now. As the road climbed higher, she looked for a broken handrail she'd noticed earlier. There it was. And there was the street sign. Stonehurst.

It was too soon. Much too soon. If only she had met Jeremy in Albany, or at least under normal circumstances, she would have invited him in, and they could really talk and get to know each other.

"I'm staying at the house on the corner," she said. "The one with two flights of stairs and the ship's model over the door."

She hadn't noticed until then that Jeremy had pulled back and slowed. Now he stopped. "You're staying at the Shenley house?" His question sounded like an accusation.

"I don't know the name of the people who own it. We're only taking it for the bicentennial. I understand the woman who owns it has been ill, and the steps were getting to be too much for her. She's staying with her daughter until..." Confusion robbed her of her speech. Was it anger she read in his face? Surprise? Had he actually paled, or was it the eerie glow of the street lantern?

"You're here with Natalie Kerr."

"How did you know?"

"Talk about the reunion has gone on for months. Who'll be coming in from where and where they'll be staying."

"And you know Natalie?"

"Does that surprise you?" The strangeness of his tone made prickles rise on her skin.

"I suppose not. Doesn't everybody know everybody else in Sandgate?" The lightness in her voice didn't work. The moments of magic had flown, and they both knew it.

A foghorn sounded, and Jeremy looked in the direction of the sea. "You just *happened* to come to Eli's shack."

"Yes, I've told you. Some children sent me."

"You didn't come looking for me?"

"What are you suggesting?"

"Don't you know?"

"Will you stop talking in riddles? What's wrong? If you know Natalie, and there are hard feelings between you, surely you could—"

"Hard feelings? No."

"Then, I don't—"

"I believe I'll forgo those stairs," he said tersely, taking an unsteady step backward to put distance between them. "You can make your way from here alone."

"Of course, I can." She wanted to ask about their plans for the next morning. Were they still on? No. How could they be?

"I'll watch to see that you get safely into the house."

A burning behind her eyes warned Melissa that she might cry. She mustn't. "Don't bother," she snapped. "We're in the upright, uptight, honorable village of Sandgate, remember? How could anything unpleasant possibly happen to me here?"

She glanced back as she reached the front door and opened it, but Jeremy turned abruptly, without a parting signal, and disappeared into the mist. The black dog trotted after him.

Well, she thought philosophically, fighting back the fey sadness that clutched at her. Everyone had a bittersweet memory or two of the man who got away. And nine out of ten times, it was for the best.

"Wherever have you been?" Natalie's voice was strident. "Jean has been impossible, fretting over you."

This, Melissa didn't need. "I was walking on the beach."

"In this fog?" The woman pressed two fingers to the bridge of her nose. "Good heavens. Your clothes. Were you walking on the beach or rolling on it?"

Melissa considered a reply appropriate to her own troubled mood, but rejected it. "A bit of both. It's worn me out."

"I'm not surprised." Natalie waited at the foot of the stairs as Melissa started up. There was only a yellowish light in the narrow hallway and with her hair drawn back and her slim body draped in her stark black robe, she looked like the menacing housekeeper in an amateur production of *Rebecca*. "I do hope no one saw you. People here tend to frown on the, shall we say, carefree style of dress. Sandgate is not tolerant."

Sandgate. Sandgate. Melissa gritted her teeth and kept climbing the stairs. "It was hard for me to see my own hand in front of my face in the fog. I don't think I've disgraced you."

"Melissa?"

"Yes?" Now what?

"Jean is determined that you accompany us to the dance tomorrow evening. It's to be an elegant affair, and the finest families will be in attendance. Do—do you have anything to wear?"

There was something so ludicrous about the woman's anxious face, Melissa almost laughed. Natalie was terrified that she would tag along to their fancy ball clad in tatters.

"I have something suitable."

"Splendid." The woman's tight smile said she wasn't convinced. "I'll say good-night then. Please don't disturb your sister. I want her fresh and rested in the morning."

Catching her own reflection in the mirror at the top of the stairs, Melissa groaned. Her hostess had good reason to fret. She looked a fright. Her hair was streaming. Her clothes were soiled, and her face was pale. It was little wonder Jeremy York thought better of his impetuous invitation to spend the day together. She likely wouldn't see him again. He'd expressed a definite disdain for the festivities and hadn't bothered to attend the opening-night banquet.

"Don't mind Nat," someone said.

Startled, Melissa spun around to see Brian standing near the window of the room she'd passed, smoking a cigarette in the darkness. He crushed it out and came toward her.

"I don't mind her," Melissa said. "Much. But I'll have a celebration of my own when all this is over."

"Don't judge the whole community by my sister."

"I'm not," she assured him, remembering with chagrin the changeable Mr. York and his uppity talk of private beaches and privileged natives. If only she hadn't leapt so eagerly at his invitation, she might have kept a little more of her pride intact.

"I have a fantastic idea." Brian pressed a hand against the wall above her head and looked down at her through a thick fringe of amber lashes. "There's a heap of history hereabouts, and I'd like someone to tour with. Tomorrow morning, we'll rise with the sun, toss together a picnic lunch and see everything there is to see."

Somehow the suggestion didn't tickle her fancy. "Everything?"

He shrugged one shoulder. "You're absolutely right. We should save something for the next day."

She squeezed her eyes closed for several seconds, trying to keep her mind on the conversation, when part of it kept drifting back to Jeremy and his strange attitude. "I wouldn't want to take you away from your fellow Sandgators."

"Sandgators?" His grin made his eyes crinkle boyishly. "You make them sound like a collection of giant lizards."

"In some cases," she said tightly, "the comparison is probably fitting." The light was out in her sister's room. She could tell by the hefty crack under the door. It was time for her to make a brave attempt at sleep herself. She turned toward her room.

"What about the picnic?" Brian reminded her.

"Picnic?" How could she turn him down without hurting his feelings? But her disappointing evening had stolen away her taste for exploring, at least temporarily. "I don't think so. I should get my hair done for the dance."

"Oh, Melissa." He made a clicking sound with his tongue. "You are magnificent."

"Why is it I don't feel magnificent?" she asked, knowing perfectly well what kind of picture she made.

"You really don't know how luscious you are, do you? You're one little lady who doesn't have to twist, bake and spray the life out of a glorious head of hair. Just wear it loose, the way you wore it when I first saw you, and I guarantee, you'll take everyone's breath away."

"Thank you, sir. I needed those encouraging words more than you know."

He touched her shoulder again, curving his fingers around it to draw her closer. "Then the picnic's on?"

"I don't think so." She liked Brian, and if tonight, meeting Jeremy, hadn't happened, she might have welcomed such an outing. But it had happened. "Have you seen the list of reunion activities Natalie posted on the door?"

"I've seen it."

"There are so many parties and dances my head is spinning. And I don't know how many of them I'll be expected to attend."

Downstairs, Natalie could be heard clicking off lights, closing windows and making going-to-bed noises. In a moment she'd be up. Brian was probably thinking the same thing. He edged closer but years of evading unwelcome familiarities alerted Melissa that she was about to be kissed.

"Good night," she said brightly, making a quick pivot that took her out of Brian's grasp.

"I'll be up with the sun anyhow," he said. "Just in case you change your mind."

"I won't," she promised. "Good night."

CHAPTER FOUR

THOUGH SHE'D EXPECTED to be troubled by dreams of giant Tilt-O-Whirls and hurtling roller coasters, her sleep was surprisingly sound. The house was so still the squawk of the cuckoo clock on the landing seemed calculated to berate her for staying so long in bed.

"Up with the sun," she muttered on her way to the washroom, noticing that Brian's bedroom door was still closed.

It was just as well. She'd have an excuse to prowl about on her own. The itinerary Natalie had posted told her that before the dance there would be a round of open house teas, allowing people to visit wherever they pleased and get reacquainted if they were out of towners.

Surely Melissa wouldn't be missed. A note slipped under her sister's door would explain her whereabouts.

After donning khaki pants and a shirt for practical hiking, she tied a kelly-green scarf at her throat to add a cheery dash of color. With her hair secured by a green ribbon and a braided string belt about her waist, she was ready.

The sight of Natalie scribbling away at the desk in the living room took her by surprise. The heavy silence pervading the house had made her believe the woman was a late sleeper.

"Oh!" She paused with a hand on the banister. "Good morning."

Natalie whisked jeweled glasses off the end of her nose. "Not off again so early? You haven't even had breakfast."

"It's difficult to stay in bed when there are so many things to see and do," Melissa said, puzzling at the woman's unexpected solicitude.

"If you'd only wait a few moments, I'm sure Brian will be up and about. He can go with you." Natalie smiled, but the frown line between her eyebrows remained. "Wait. I'll call him."

"I'd rather you didn't." Now she understood. After last night's escapade, Natalie was convinced that Melissa needed someone to keep her out of trouble. "Your brother has far better things to do than to look after me."

"He would want me to wake him," the woman insisted, moving toward the stairway.

"I'll be back in plenty of time for the dance," Melissa promised, weary of the argument. She called back from the doorway. "Enjoy your day."

She didn't need Jeremy—or Brian. The sky was clear blue, the air was fresh, and the sun was brilliant. There was just the flutter of a breeze to play with the strands of ebony hair that had escaped the green ribbon.

She'd search the shops on her own. Antiques had always been a special weakness of Melissa's. Not priced-out-of-sight spindly-legged chairs that had once belonged to King Someone-or-Other. But bits of costume jewelry, kitchen hangables from years past and glassy-eyed dolls with frizzled hair.

She was in luck and discovered a charming little place with dusty corners, cluttered trays and a proprietor who didn't shadow her and try to sell her the contents of the shop. She bought only a glass paperweight, one with a snowstorm inside. So thoroughly immersed was she in her search that the morning flew.

She wasn't hungry, and she wasn't yet ready to go back to the house. Not with the sea calling to her from below. There was real satisfaction in a lazy, unhurried day such as this one, when she had no one to please but herself.

When she had made her way down to the sand, she perched on a rock and sat, contentedly watching the herring gulls take their turns at plunging into the foaming breakers. If only she had thought to buy a sketch pad and charcoal, she could capture the scene on her own terms and keep the memory for other times.

It was a solitary spot. She was alone. Yet the feeling that came with aloneness didn't touch her. She had the sensation of being watched, though there was no one about. Or was there? Eli's shack was out of sight, somewhere to her right and up, obscured by rocks, dunes and stunted trees bent low by years of wind and storm. Two other people sat on the sand some distance up the beach. A man and a child of about four. But they were too occupied with building a sand castle to take notice of her.

First scanning the stretch of smooth beach to the other side, Melissa shaded her eyes and looked toward the ledge above. Her pulses began pounding out a deafening fugue when she saw a man standing on the rocky shelf, staring down at her. It was Jeremy. But the recognition did nothing to relieve her apprehension.

The breeze tousled his dark hair and clearly patterned his shirt and slacks to the strong male lines of his body. Even at a distance she could see the fierce set of his features—or did she imagine it?

Determined not to be intimidated by him, she smiled and waved a hand in exaggerated greeting, as she might have done if they were old chums happening upon each other in welcome surprise. She should be sketching, like some otherwise idle Victorian woman, and he would make his way down to admire the way she had transferred what she saw to paper.

"It's so much more than a mere copy," he would say, completely awed by her talent. "You've managed to capture not only what I see when I stand in this spot but what I feel."

The real Jeremy wasn't so cooperative. He didn't return her wave or show any sign of recognition. But he didn't move away, either.

The child's cry distracted her. She turned toward the sound. The father was trying to introduce his unwilling son to the chill water, and the child was wailing and clinging to his legs.

"Don't be such a baby," the man was chiding. "There aren't any fish out there big enough to eat you."

When she turned her attention to the ledge again, Jeremy was gone. But where?

She studied the narrow shelf for many moments with a curiosity bordering on excitement, finding the place where it cut into the hill face and made steps, of a sort, upward. Did he live up there somewhere?

She could visualize him in a cabin similar to Eli's, more sparsely furnished, but just as cluttered. He'd have a crudely made slab desk, where he'd sit long hours, combing restless fingers through his crisp black hair as he plotted some new mechanical thrill for fairgoers everywhere.

Before she had time to rethink her actions, the child in her lured her toward the slope. Hoping to catch a glimpse of the cabin she had already furnished in her mind, she began working a diagonal path between the low boulders, pushing aside some of the dry, wind-whipped branches and ducking under others.

Enthusiasm for her adventure dimmed as she reached the halfway point and realized, even if it meant being seen, she should have chosen an easier ascent. The rise that lay before her was precipitous and threateningly brambled. It was time for a retreat.

Too late. Her foot slid between two close-set stones as she turned, pitching her forward. Her arms flailed wildly as she tried for a handhold. Any handhold. She caught a limb, but it gave way with a thunderous cracking sound as it split to the root. It cushioned her fall but left her facedown, her hair caught in the angry snarl of branches.

Groaning in frustration rather than pain, she lay very still, wanting to make certain she wasn't hurt.

"Are you all right?" A man's voice boomed from above her.

If it was Jeremy, she decided, making claws of the fingers that pressed into the gravelly earth, she wouldn't answer. She'd stay there until he moved away. He couldn't see her, and he might think he'd imagined the noise.

"Dammit, answer me. Are you hurt?"

It was Jeremy. She recognized the snarl. "I'm fine," she called. "Will you please go away?"

"What the devil are you doing?" He was closer now.

"I'm studying flora and fauna," she snapped, trying with frantic manipulations to free her hair.

"Hold on. Let me do that." His knee dug into her rib cage as his fingers began working at her hair. "We can't save the ribbon, I'm afraid."

"Ouch! Forget the ribbon. Just save the hair, won't you?"

"Sorry. There you go. Up now." Tugging at her with an awkward hold that brought her up bottom first, he set her upright, steadying her against his own body.

Sharply aware of the intimacy of her position, she stepped away and began brushing furiously at her pants. They were ripped from calf to knee. Ruined on their first wearing. She could have screamed.

"You've scratched your face," he said, reaching out.

She shrank from his touch, pressing a finger to the stinging place she'd only that moment noticed alongside of her chin. "It's nothing."

"All in a day's adventure, I suppose." His eyes were gleaming jet stones.

"I like to hike."

"You might have tried the path."

"I was on my way to Eli's cabin."

"You're off course."

"I guessed as much." How could such a monosyllabic exchange unnerve her? she wondered, feeling the sudden need to escape.

"I'm going there myself," he said. "I'll take you."

"Oh, no." Ignoring the hand Jeremy offered, she brushed the hair from her forehead to clear her vision and dropped to her knees again. The paperweight. She'd lost it in her struggle for balance.

"Now what?"

"You go ahead," she told him, patting the thick tussocks of wild grass and reaching into a small hollow that angled downward.

"What are you looking for?"

There it was. She curled her fingers around the glassy smoothness and drew her treasure carefully from its hiding place, grateful that it hadn't shattered. "My paperweight."

"You carry a paperweight with you?" He sounded disbelieving, as if he thought she was somehow bent on invading his sacrosanct hillside.

"Yes," she answered, bristling. "No. It's actually a miniature camera. I'm a spy, you see, and the entire world is breathlessly awaiting news of the Sandgate reunion festivities."

His half smile was just as charming as it had been before, maybe even more so with golden spears of afternoon sunlight touching his bronzed skin. But she wasn't charmed. She'd seen the less-than-disarming side of Mr. Jeremy York the night before and had been hurt by it.

"Maybe I should search you for hidden microfilm."

"Maybe you'd like to try." The second she'd uttered the ill-advised challenge, she regretted it.

His focus lowered to her breasts, and every inch of her from tip to toe was flushed with an uncomfortable warmth. "No need," he said. "A visual search is more than adequate."

Her intake of breath was almost a hiccough as she glanced down to see that it wasn't only her pants that were torn. Her shirt was minus its buttons and open to the waist, showing a sheer pink bra and an even pinker expanse of skin.

Jeremy laughed at her discomfort. "Such modesty. You'd be revealing more than that on the beach in your average bikini."

"I don't wear a bikini," she lied.

"A pity."

"May we go now?" she asked crisply, yanking the
ends of her shirt together to tie them in a secure knot.

"Of course."

His was a beautifully formed back, she thought, not
able to keep from noticing the symmetrical knit of his
muscles—here, there, everywhere. His was also a
handsome back-of-head. Nonsense, she chided herself.
What could be special about the back of anyone's head?
Still . . .

Jarring her thoughts to safer ground, she inserted bits
of nervous conversation into the ensuing silence, telling him about her search of the antique shops that
morning and about her luck in finding the paperweight.

"And your business in Westerly. How did it go?" she
asked, wanting him to know she hadn't forgotten his
invitation, offered and withdrawn. Perhaps he'd even
explain and clear the air between them.

"About as I expected." With an exaggerated sweep
of one hand, he held a drooping branch aside. As if she
could have become any more disheveled by pushing her
own way through.

"Thank you," she said, disappointment making her
voice barely audible.

"There's Eli's cabin." He pointed. "I still don't see
how you missed your way. The landmarks are clear.
There's the Sea View."

"It was foggy last night, remember?"

"All the more reason for—"

"Is it really so important?" She slid past him to take
the lead, wanting to sidestep the question before he had
time to realize what had actually lured her up the slope.
"If I'm going to meet Eli, I'd better do it. The dance is

tonight, and I have to get back in time to make myself presentable.''

Eli Campbell wasn't shy and standoffish, as she had expected he would be. He wasn't even particularly surprised by her visit, and if her less-than-elegant appearance took him aback, he didn't comment on it. He was in his late fifties, with pale eyes, thinning iron-gray hair and a firm handclasp that didn't match the frailty of his physical makeup. His plaid shirt and well-worn dungarees hung on him as if he had shrunk inside them.

"Come to see Murphy, have you?"

"Murphy?" she questioned.

"I'm a believer in the name suiting the owner. Murphy means 'warrior of the sea,' and it fits him like his feathers. Took a liking to Ilona, his cage mate, right off. Won't let any of the others near her."

"You give names to all the birds you doctor?"

"Everything with a heart that beats deserves its own identity." In pushing aside a pile of unopened letters, he swept several to the floor but didn't bother to retrieve them. He plucked a frayed account book out of the desk clutter and waved it.

"They're all of them in here. And I've treated almost as many little winged creatures over the years as there are grains of sand on the beach. I make note of all of them. Even those unfortunate fellows I can't save. Come along." He sniffed. "I'll show you my present boarders. Some of them are about to strike out on their own again."

"Just give me a minute to put myself together," Melissa said apologetically. "I slipped on your hillside, I'm afraid."

Eli nodded. "The washroom is through that door."

"She knows the way," Jeremy commented, digging the coffee tin out of the kitchen cabinet above the sink. "She ran afoul of the terrain yesterday, too."

Without a lipstick, a hasty washing was the best Melissa could do for her face. A rubber band she found on Eli's doorknob served to hold her hair back, and a strategically placed safety pin, also borrowed from her host, kept the ripped pant leg from ripping further. She wrinkled her nose at her unglamorous mirror image. What did it matter how she looked? Murphy wouldn't care.

The tour of the bird hospital was an enjoyable one, with Doctor Eli enthusiastically commenting on this or that bird and explaining how each had come to him. There was Keegan, meaning "fiery one," and Asta, meaning "star," and Irving, meaning "friend from the sea." So many of them.

"We'll be fast friends, Melissa," Eli promised her. "And that's good. I can use an extra pair of hands these days. Jeremiah, show her how to feed those little ones, won't you? Then we can busy ourselves with fixing that broken shelf for Gallagher and Frey."

Jeremiah? Melissa considered the name and wondered if it truly belonged to Jeremy, or if it was a jovial tag Eli had placed on him. Somehow it fit. What did it mean? she wondered.

A covered bowl Jeremy removed from the refrigerator was filled with what appeared to be dog food. He added liquid, dipped into the mixture with a toothpick and made tweeting sounds as he eased the food toward the nest of baby birds, whose beaks opened laughably wide as he approached. Gone was the straight-backed guardian of the gates. Here was a gentle man whose tenderness almost brought tears to her eyes.

"This is the way. You see? They'll think you're their mama. Let's see you do it."

"I'm not sure I can," she protested, drawing back as he pressed a toothpick into her hand. The tiny creatures, all pink and featherless, would be so easily injured.

"Go ahead." Firmly he placed a hand on one of her shoulders, so close she could feel the warmth of his breath on her cheek.

She inhaled sharply and was catapulted into action, her hand trembling as she imitated Jeremy's movements. What if she were to push too hard, too far? "Like this?"

"Perfect. Congratulations. You have a job."

It was a rewarding task, but a lengthy one. By the time Melissa had satisfied her hungry brood, Jeremy had finished his sawing and hammering in the walk-in cage. How he accomplished anything at all, though, she couldn't fathom. The entire time he worked, the two men argued good-naturedly, but in earnest. Jeremy thought Eli was doing too much on his first day out of hospital. Eli thought Jeremy was all wet. Lying in bed, he claimed, was what did a man in, not honest toil. Unable to keep from laughing at the stinging barbs they exchanged, Melissa set to work changing papers in the bottoms of the cages and filling water and feed dishes.

At last the three sat down for biscuits and mugs of Jeremy's abominable coffee, and Eli told about how his interest in birds began.

When it was time to go Melissa promised, "I'll be back again soon."

"You're welcome anytime, young lady," Eli assured her, following her to the door. "Anytime. But you,

Jeremiah—stay away. I don't want you running your legs off doing for me. I'll be fine."

"I'll see you tomorrow," Jeremy said.

"Not if I see you first," Eli said, cackling. "I can do better without your fussing over me."

Something in the way the older man had ushered Jeremy out with Melissa left her with the distinct impression that Eli was trying to play matchmaker. It was a bit embarrassing, but she didn't mind too much. She'd seen another side to Jeremy York's nature that day. A side she liked. Maybe they'd gotten off on the wrong foot before, as people do, and here was the perfect opportunity to make up for it. The walk home at a leisurely pace might take fifteen minutes. Much could be accomplished in a short time if two people were bent on getting to know each other.

A flash of gray and a bird's cry overhead caught their attention, and they stood together for a moment, watching the flight.

"I wonder if he's one of Eli's graduates," Melissa said.

"Maybe."

She wanted to ask him about Eli. The man's hermit life-style puzzled her almost as much as she had been puzzled when she'd supposed Jeremy was the birdman. Eli was a warm, giving person, who seemed to be starving for companionship. He certainly must have conversed with his "little people," as he called his patients, when no one else was about. A friend, if he were truly a friend, would have long ago encouraged him to put his grief behind him and venture out to take his place in the world again.

Before she had time to put her thoughts into words, Jeremy turned to her, and she sensed that he was going to say something profound. The waiting made her feel as if she were inching out on the limb of a tall tree. Without warning, the limb might break and she would fall, twisting and turning, if he didn't reach out to her.

"Do you have your paperweight?"

Instead of answering, she held it up and shook it, making the snow fall inside the little glass ball.

"Good. Can you find your way all right from here?" he asked.

"Yes, of course." She tried not to sound as dismayed as she felt.

"You're sure?" He frowned.

"Very sure," she said through clamped teeth, wondering if this should be considered a second rejection or only a continuation of the first.

"I'll say goodbye then."

"Goodbye," she echoed, starting down the beach.

So much for their nice getting-to-know-each-other chat, she thought, feeling his eyes burning into her as she went on her way. Or perhaps he wasn't watching her at all. Perhaps he'd already started up the hill.

Fortunately, Natalie's back was turned to the door when Melissa arrived home, and she was able to scurry up the stairs without being seen. The woman would have been appalled by her appearance this time. Her sister's door was ajar, and the girl was lying on the bed, staring at the ceiling. She sat up abruptly and swung her feet onto the floor when she saw Melissa. Apparently all was not well.

"You were right," Arlene wailed, ushering her inside the bedroom. "This entire charade was a horrendous mistake. Natalie is the female version of Attila the Hun. Look!"

As far as Melissa could see, there was no problem. Unless it was the evening dress that hung on the closet door. It was lacy and pink with a full skirt and puffed sleeves. "She bought you some clothes? How nice."

"Nice? Would you like to wear this?" Arlene yanked the dress from its hanger and held it under her chin. "I'm being 'allowed' to wear my turquoise to the dance tonight, she says. There isn't time to do any more shopping. But my clothes are far too sophisticated for my piano recital at the big talent show Friday night. Too sophisticated!"

Melissa suppressed a groan. "Maybe the dress isn't what you would have chosen, baby. But you're Jean Kerr for now, remember? You're only supposed to be seventeen. Natalie thinks the dress will make you look younger."

"I don't look younger in this atrocity. I look stupid and ugly." The girl's lower lip began to quiver.

Usually Melissa could have stopped her sister's flow of tears with a few carefully selected words of encouragement. It was just such an episode—perhaps one of many—she had foreseen when she insisted on coming to Sandgate. Arlene could be sailing on a cloud one moment and plunging into the depths of despair the next. When called on it later, the girl would laugh and blame it on her artistic nature.

At this moment, however, Melissa didn't feel much like a peacemaker. The words wouldn't come. She sighed and shook her head.

"If these strangers frown on your fashion sense, what difference will it make? When we leave here, we'll never see any of them again."

"But we will. I met somebody at the banquet last night. And I saw him again today, when Natalie and I were shopping." Arlene dropped the offending gown onto a chair and settled cross-legged on the bed, plucking a tissue from its box to blow her nose. "A very special somebody."

So that was it. Arlene was always meeting somebody. "You haven't known whoever-he-is long enough to care very much about him. You can't even have made a true judgment of his character."

"Oh?" The girl raised her chin and looked down the length of her nose. "You're a fine one to talk, after what you've been up to."

"I don't know what you mean."

"Miss Innocent. You've only met Brian a couple of times, and if that wasn't Romeo and Juliet I heard outside my door last night, I'll eat that dress, ruffles and all."

"You should have lived in another age, baby sister. You can see romance in a pepperoni pizza."

Her sister flopped back on the pillow and patted a place beside her on the bed. "Let me tell you about the man I met. Todd's witty and handsome and sincere, and—"

"Enough chatter." Melissa decided against worrying. Her sister fell out of love more quickly than she fell in. So far no male had ever been around long enough to take the place of her first love—music. "I don't know how I'll ever get ready in time for the dance as it is."

"I knew I could count on you." The younger girl's face looked especially pixieish when her hair was done in all-over ribbon curlers. She also looked a mite smug.

Melissa froze with a hand on the door. "Count on me for what?"

"To fix it with Natalie so I don't have to wear that horrid Goldilocks costume for the piano recital."

"Arlene!"

"Shh!" The girl pressed a finger to her lips. "I'm Jean, remember? And you'd better get moving. You do look a fright."

CHAPTER FIVE

"SO JEAN DOESN'T CARE for the dress we chose together when we were shopping?" Natalie asked, fluttering her fingers to dry her freshly applied nail polish.

"She feels that it's too young for her. Frankly, I agree."

"How odd." The woman lifted one spidery thin eyebrow. She'd already applied her makeup, and her eyelids were glittery and golden. "It wasn't until she consulted with you that she decided it wasn't right."

"She didn't want to hurt your feelings."

"How sweet." Natalie laughed, but there was no mirth in it. "You've always made decisions for her, haven't you? It must be extremely painful to see her grow away from you."

Melissa felt a warming through her cheeks. It meant her color was rising along with her temper. "The tags are still attached to the dress. If you have the receipt there shouldn't be any trouble with returning it. If you like, I'd be glad to handle it for you."

"I'm sure you would. You want her to believe that any choice she makes without you is wrong."

"That's nonsense. If you'd only—"

"Naturally I cannot force her to wear the dress. You've won. This time." Natalie's voice rose dramatically to drown out Melissa's protest. "But from now on, kindly remember that you are an uninvited guest in this house. Stop your meddling.''

"What you're suggesting is—"

"I will not hear any more.'' The woman rose, pressing her hands to her temples. "I will not allow you to upset me tonight of all nights.''

"I'm not trying to—"

"Ladies!'' Brian burst through the door as if he were in a play and someone had just given him his cue. It was an obvious attempt at rescue. The gaiety in his voice by no means matched the concern in his eyes. "Time grows short. Hadn't you better slip into your finery?''

"I'm not given to violence,'' Melissa murmured when Natalie had flitted past and up the stairs. "But in another minute, I'd have grabbed her and shaken out all the hairpins from that elegant hairdo.''

"Another time, kitten,'' he said, "and I'd pay admission to see it. But tonight . . . the show must go on.''

"What am I doing here?''

"You're being a caring sister and a good friend. Can you try and pretend none of this happened? For your sister's sake?''

Melissa squeezed the hand that reached for hers. "I can try.''

"Good girl.''

Melissa made her way upstairs and was on her way to her room when Arlene's door opened a crack. "Wear your white,'' the girl sang.

"I'd planned to wear my green.''

"Please. I'm wearing my turquoise and we'd clash. Besides, you look smashing in white. Natalie's gown is black and it'll be a study in contrasts.''

"Will she wear her peaked hat and carry her broom, too?''

Arlene drew herself up and sniffed. "How dare you say such thing about my dear, darling mother."

"Easily." Melissa sighed. "Who leads whom around by the nose?"

"How's that again?"

"Never mind, pet. I'll see you later."

Melissa's white dress was a perfect fit, and as usual Arlene was right. It was more daring than anything else she owned, but it was very becoming. It bared one smooth golden shoulder and its side splits showed a ladylike but tantalizing expanse of shapely leg as she walked. The starkness of the clinging crepe de chine made her hair look raven and brought out the jade green of her eyes.

She and her sister emerged from their rooms simultaneously and showered compliments on each other. The younger girl's hair was a gleaming cap of curls. Her turquoise dress was styled like a Roman toga. Her shoes were silvery straps, and a wide band of silver circled her waist. She looked more beautiful than Melissa had ever seen her look before.

Natalie looked very glamorous, too, Melissa had to admit. The black dress fit like a second skin until it flared at the knee. She didn't have an excess ounce. Her golden hair, slick and smooth, was fastened with an outsized clip of gold and pearls.

Brian, looking dashing in a white dinner jacket and tie, gave a low appreciative whistle.

"You aren't so bad yourself, Unc," Arlene said, tickling him under the chin. "Be sure and save a dance for your poor little old niece."

"If I can fight my way through the mob of admirers."

The car wound inland through meadowland and woods until it turned through a gateway, where a guard in a booth took their names and allowed them entrance. At the end of a tree-lined driveway sat the house, every window ablaze with lights. When they got out of the car, a red-jacketed young man whisked it out of sight. Strains of "Smoke Gets in your Eyes" drew them up the flagstone path to the wide porch.

Natalie, guiding her "daughter" before her, put on a gleaming smile and swept through the open doors, hugging and kissing everyone in sight. Brian and Melissa tagged behind, left to their own devices.

The hostess was a woman in her sixties with dark, silver-streaked hair and very white skin. The enormous emerald pendant she wore and her vivid green dress only accentuated her pallor. "Natalie," she said. "You haven't changed a whit."

"Why, thank you, Mrs. Havelock," Natalie gushed, though Melissa would have bet, judging from the older woman's flat tone, that she hadn't meant the remark as a compliment.

"She's lovely," Mrs. Havelock pronounced, when Natalie presented her temporary daughter. Then she peered through her silver-rimmed glasses at Melissa. "And this is another of your girls?"

"No. Oh, no. Melissa Brandon is a visitor in our midst. She's in Sandgate as a guest of my brother, Brian. You'd hardly remember Brian, of course. He was so young when we moved."

Feeling as she did about Melissa, Natalie would have been outraged at being taken for her mother. The outrage showed itself in her too-rapid protests.

Melissa dug her fingernails into the palms of her hands to keep from smiling too broadly at Natalie's discomfort. She didn't dare to look at Brian. If she did, she would probably burst out laughing.

When she had composed herself enough to look around, she realized that her sister had disappeared. The girl had slipped into the milling crowd. Natalie would be chewing her fingernails when she noticed her absence.

Melissa stretched herself as tall as she could and tried to peer over the heads of the people who stood in her line of vision between the entranceway and the ballroom. It was then that she looked directly into Jeremy's eyes. For an electrifying moment she was stunned into silence.

A tingling began in her fingers and toes, then spiraled up her arms and legs to center in the pit of her stomach. She implored her sense of humor to come to her rescue, and it didn't fail her. All this was no more than an elaborate stage set, she reminded herself. Everyone was comically miscast. Most of all, Natalie, who was acting the oh, so doting mother, and Brian, who looked painfully uncomfortable in his starched collar and bow tie. Melissa herself was reacting as a smitten teenager might over a man she hardly knew. She and Arlene would have myriad things to laugh about later, when all this was over.

"Jeremy, my dear," Mrs. Havelock called. "Natalie's here."

Gravely, he walked over and took one of Natalie's hands. "It's been a long time."

"Too long." It was clear from the breathless quality in Natalie's voice and in the lingering glances the two exchanged that they had known each other more than casually.

"The other young woman," Mrs. Havelock continued, "is Melissa Brandon. She's come to share in the fun with us."

"Miss Brandon and I have met," he said, scanning her as though he had been called upon to guess her weight. "But I must admit I hardly recognized her."

"You look very different yourself," she countered, deciding that she liked him better the other way. He looked more than a little pompous. His dark hair, attractively shaggy and windblown before, was combed neatly, and his casual denim shirt had been exchanged for a dinner jacket and tie.

Sparks flew from Natalie's eyes. "You didn't tell me you'd made friends on your nocturnal stroll, Melissa."

"There was a wounded bird on the beach. Mr. York helped me with it."

"How like Jeremy. Always befriending poor unfortunates." Natalie glanced around then, discovering for the first time that one of their party was missing. Petulance crept into her voice and caused her fun-loving image to slip another notch. "Now where has my daughter gone? I wanted you to meet her."

"She's dancing," Mrs. Havelock said. "Didn't you see Todd spirit her away?"

"No. She didn't say anything to me." Nervously, Natalie's eyes darted to the dance floor. "Yes. There she is. The girl in the blue-green dress. Do you see her, Jeremy? Isn't she breathtaking?"

Jeremy looked first at Melissa, then to the dance floor. "Your daughter's quite beautiful."

"Thank you. But don't tell me that very tall young man is Todd—your little brother? I can't believe it. He was only a child when I last saw him."

Jeremy didn't answer. All his attention was focused on the dancers.

"They're playing a Cole Porter medley," Natalie cooed, tugging at his arm. "Let's not let it go to waste."

"You do something to me," Brian said to Melissa under his breath.

"What?"

"The song they're playing. 'You Do Something to Me.' Shall we dance, too?"

"If you like."

The ballroom was circular with a magnificent crystal chandelier in the center of the high, curved ceiling. Between each of the many windows was a gilt and mahogany-framed mirror, reflecting the swaying dancers again and again, magnifying the size of the already gigantic room. Through glass doors lay a kind of greenhouse with vines, hanging plants and trees everywhere. Long tables had been set up, laden with every imaginable delicacy. It was a feast Melissa would have dug into with enthusiasm another time. Tonight she had little appetite. Why had Jeremy led her to believe that he wouldn't be here?

He and Natalie made an attractive couple, she admitted grudgingly. They moved together as if they were professional dancers, going through a well-practiced routine. Though they carried on a conversation all the while, they didn't miss a step.

"You didn't tell me you'd met York." Brian's comment held a definite bite.

"When did I have the chance to tell you? There's been so much going on. Does it matter?"

"I wonder. You aren't able to keep your eyes off him."

Melissa fastened Brian with a sharp look. "I'm only surprised to see him here. He expressed a definite dislike for these celebrations."

"He could hardly stay away. Mrs. Havelock is his mother-in-law. This is her party, though it's being held in his house."

His mother-in-law? Her jaw slackened at the impact of Brian's remark. She might have known Jeremy was married. It explained the sudden change in his manner and his reason for withdrawing his invitation when he learned she was with Natalie. Closeness didn't make for comfortable philandering.

And she'd thought of him as warm and caring, as down-to-earth and human. Hah. That was why love at first sight rarely grew as it did in storybooks. You met someone and something about his voice, his face, his walk—or the way he laughed—settled into your heart. You began to flesh out all the unknown vacant places with bits of your own fantasy. Before you knew it, you were hopelessly enamored of a fairy-tale prince who existed only in your imagination, and you wondered why he appeared to be changing.

Why couldn't Jeremy York have truly been Eli Campbell?

"You're surprised that he's married, aren't you?" Brian asked carefully.

"Yes. He struck me as a born bachelor."

"You've formed some strong opinions about a man you met only briefly."

"I have a tendency to do that." Melissa trapped her lower lip between her teeth. *Brian, please,* she begged silently. *I don't need you to change, too.* "Is he the one who walked out on Natalie?" she asked slowly, already fearing the answer. "The one you told me about?"

"The same. Poor Nat didn't have a chance. Wealth makes for tough competition."

"You're saying he married for money?"

"What do you think?" He paused, letting his words sink in. "Oh, not because he was poor. Not by a long shot. But money is a powerful drug. The more these people have, the more they covet. The Yorks made theirs in shipping. In case you didn't know, that's a euphemism. It began with smuggling not so many generations back. Now it's all very legal. Steel, plastics—"

"He told me he builds amusement park rides."

"That's his own personal baby. He took a gamble, and it paid off. But what kind of gamble was it? If he'd lost a million or two, he wouldn't have felt it."

"You don't like him?"

Brian looked down at her. "You could say that I'm jealous."

"Does money mean so much to you?"

"It isn't the money that makes me jealous." The arm that circled her waist tightened, drawing her so close against him that she could scarcely breathe. "It's what I see in your face when you look at him that's got me worried."

"You're imagining things."

"I don't think so." His voice was getting loud.

"Brian, people are beginning to look at us."

"If I'm imagining things, prove it. Let's take a drive. This place is claustrophobic. Nat would understand. We've put in an appearance. That's all she expects."

"I can't."

"Can't or won't?"

"I promised my sister."

"Her again."

"Please try to understand," she pleaded, trailing after him as he pushed his way none too gently through the maze of dancers.

Poor Brian, she thought. Natalie's attitude and playacting had unnerved him, too, and made him ready to leap down anyone's throat at the slightest provocation. He hadn't meant anything he said. She would have gone after him to smooth his feathers if Arlene hadn't popped up at that moment with her young man in tow.

"Melissa, meet Todd. Todd, meet Melissa," she chirped, pushing them together. "Dance, won't you? I want you to get to know each other. Where's Uncle Brian off to in such a huff? I want to collect the dance he promised." Before Melissa could object, she sailed away.

Todd might have been very nice. But there was too much of a family resemblance for her to appraise his qualities objectively. He was slimmer and years younger, but his eyes were Jeremy's eyes, and his full, finely molded mouth was Jeremy's mouth. Even his voice was similar.

He made polite conversation about her job, about the weather and other routine subjects, and she returned polite answers. But her thoughts weren't with her partner or the dance they shared. All she could do was glance about the room and wonder which of the elegantly gowned women was Jeremy's wife.

"Have you known Jean long?" Todd asked. "She thinks a lot of you. I would say the whole idea of our dancing is for me to get your approval."

"I've known her a long time, yes."

"I've never known anyone quite like her. Is she really only seventeen? She seems older."

Melissa sighed, hating this deception all over again. "She's mature for her age." It wasn't entirely a lie. Arlene was mature in some ways. In others, she was about ten years old.

"Do you play the piano, too?"

"No. I..." She sucked in her breath and held it when she saw that her sister was dancing again. Not with Brian, but with Jeremy.

Todd chuckled. "You two have a lot in common. She likes to lead, too."

Melissa mumbled an apology. In her efforts to keep out of Jeremy's way, she'd unconsciously been forcing her partner toward the other side of the dance floor.

"It's all right," he offered, grinning again. "I like a woman with a mind of her own."

A fluttering began in her middle. Her sister was trying to attract her attention. Now the two were working their way over. It would be impossible to avoid whatever the girl had in mind. I'll kill her, Melissa promised herself, cringing.

"Time to change partners. Have you met Todd's brother? Melissa, meet Jeremy. And vice versa. There now. Dance. You're old friends."

"It appears that this is our dance, like it or not," Jeremy said, taking her into his arms.

A picture of him asking her if she had a beach card flashed through her mind. It was followed closely by another vision of him on the beach, sending her on her way alone. Now he was honoring her with a dance because it had been forced on him, and nobly he was making the best of it.

"It isn't compulsory."

"But it is." His face didn't change. His voice was pleasant, as without effort he held her easily, despite her small struggle to free herself. "I see no reason to hurt Jean's feelings. She's enjoying herself."

"I'm glad someone is." Defeated, she willed herself to relax. A kick in the shins would have made him release her, and it was a temptation she would have liked to give in to. But it would have made a scene—a scene that would have spoiled her sister's time. One dance wouldn't kill her, and she'd already made it clear that she wasn't enthusiastic about being his partner.

His fingers moved at the small of her back, as expertly he guided her though one smooth step after another, steps she hadn't supposed she could do. Her flesh quivered at his touch, and a film of dampness formed on her forehead and on her upper lip. *It's only that he makes me nervous,* she reminded herself, hoping he wouldn't notice. She took a deep breath and released it slowly, trying for an air of resignation, or at least of indifference. It came out more like a sigh.

"That's better." His voice was a caress as he allowed his gaze to settle on her mouth. "You're an excellent dancer."

"Thank you," she said, deciding not to return his compliment. He already knew he was good.

Her nostrils flared involuntarily, and she turned her head dizzily to watch the other dancers when she found the little-girl romantic in her wondering how Jeremy's lips would feel on hers. They were perfect lips, wonderfully defined. They would be soft and yet firm. They would be yielding and warm—demanding. Her strength seemed to flow from her body to his. It was frightening. Again she considered breaking away. He wouldn't expect it now. He'd assume that she had fallen under his spell. She'd seek Brian out, tell him he'd been right, that she was ready to leave.

No. She wouldn't. Jeremy had a wife, and maybe she wouldn't even want him if he were free. But for the moment she could only give in to what she was feeling. The animosity she had been building up for this man who held her was evenly matched by the attraction she felt for him. She would have liked the music to go on and on.

Her limbs felt weightless as his thighs brushed hers rhythmically, again and still again. It struck her suddenly how akin dancing must be to lovemaking. A thin layer of clothing did little to prevent the heat of his body from reaching hers, as they sensed and moved to each other's movements. Trembling movements that aroused hunger without satisfying it.

"You're out of sorts because of the row you had with your friend?"

It was a jarring comment. Melissa tilted her head back to fasten him with the best glare she could muster.

"I couldn't help but notice," he added.

"If it were any of your concern, I'd answer."

"A good host makes it his business to see that everyone has a good time."

"How kind of you to sacrifice yourself to your guests' pleasure. Will every woman present be honored with a whirl around the floor with you?"

With a jerking movement, he applied pressure with the hand that guided her. It was the closest he could come to shaking her without attracting attention. His lips tightened into a straight line and his eyes narrowed in suspicion. "Why did you go to Eli's shack today?"

"I wanted to see Murphy." She made her eyes wide and fearful. "Did I trespass again? Will you make a citizen's arrest?"

"I might. If you don't behave yourself."

"Oh, I will, sir. Forgive me, sir. I'm sorry, sir."

"I thought you might have come to see me."

"If it pleases you to think that, you may."

The music stopped, but he didn't escort her from the floor. He held her as if they were still dancing, until the music started again. "I saw you on the beach before you made your climb."

"I know. I saw you, too. And you were..." Flustered by her helpless physical response to his every move, she had to fumble for the word she wanted. "You were glowering."

He laughed. "I was—what?"

"Glowering. You were glaring at me as if you planned to leap down and toss me bodily into the water."

"Was I?" His smile, not one-sided but wide and genuine this time, sent her senses reeling. Again she had to remind herself that he was a married man. It seemed that he needed reminding, as well. He was well practiced in the art of seduction and reveled in the feminine response. She'd known his type before. He was one of those contemptible men who felt it necessary to be adored. "That isn't what I was thinking of doing to you at all."

There was no denying the implication of his words or the accompanying play of his fingers at the curve of her back. That did it. Calling on all her imagination, she attempted to see, not Jeremy, but one of the obnoxious office Don Juans holding her in his arms and refusing to take no for an answer. And so she answered as she would have answered a self-styled lady-killer who had just made an obvious pass.

"Where is Mrs. York tonight?" she asked pointedly.

"My mother travels a great deal. She's in Spain now. Why do you ask?"

Melissa tasted victory. He knew which Mrs. York she meant. "I was referring to your wife. Is she here tonight? I'd like to meet her. How terribly generous she must be to share her husband's attentions with so many other women."

He didn't answer at once, but rather studied her face as if he were trying to see behind a mask she wore. "Kathryn has been dead for six years."

She couldn't have felt more shocked if he'd struck her. Her first impulse was to express her sympathy, but his unexpected answer had erased any words that might serve adequately.

"I didn't know."

"I would say we've danced enough to satisfy Jean," he said abruptly. "I'll take you back now."

When he left her at the edge of the dance floor, Melissa felt abandoned. The music was blaring. The floor was too crowded and the room too warm. A faint throbbing began in her temples. A headache wanted to start. Before she could regain her composure her sister was beside her again.

"What do you think of him?"

"I hurt his feelings."

"Todd? He didn't let on he was hurt. He thinks you're cute, in fact. Which reminds me. Hands off."

"Not Todd. Jeremy."

"I wouldn't worry about him. He's recovered. I saw him cozying up with Natalie after he left you. Personally, I think they've got something hot and heavy going, those two. Maybe he's what this trip is about."

"I wouldn't be surprised."

"Why don't you hunt Uncle Brian down?" Arlene suggested. "Get him on the dance floor. He only wants to be coaxed, poor baby."

"Maybe later. Run along and enjoy yourself."

"I plan to do just that. Natalie says I might get to perform later. A few people have asked. Be sure you try some of that greenish dip with the cauliflower around it. It's sensational."

Melissa couldn't have cared less about dip. She wanted only to escape to some dark corner until everything was over. But a balding man introduced himself and asked her to dance. Then came a banker-type who pumped her arm in time with the music, followed by a youth of about seventeen, who was somebody's grandnephew.

By the time she was able to slip away, her headache was underway in earnest. She moved past the lavish banquet tables through the double doors, down the corridor and out onto the terrace. When she discovered she still wasn't alone, she walked down the steps and followed a stone path that led past a stand of willows to a charming little gazebo beside a duck pond.

As the music grew more faint, her headache subsided proportionately. The air was sweet with the perfume of summer flowers, and there were more stars overhead than she could count.

She'd almost reached the bench beside the pond when she realized to her chagrin that the shadows to her right weren't trees. Only a few feet away stood a man and woman.

"It wasn't something I planned," the woman said huskily. "I refuse to feel guilty. Are you disappointed?"

"How could I be?" he answered.

The shock of realization rendered Melissa gelatinous. It was Jeremy and Natalie. How they'd failed to notice her already was beyond her comprehension, unless it was that they were so caught up in each other and the moment they were oblivious to all else. If only she could manage to reach the hedges, she thought frantically, she could squeeze through. She could then cut across the lawn and up the incline to the steps that would take her safely back to the terrace. She'd be home free.

"What am I going to do?" Natalie asked. "There isn't much time."

"I'll see to it."

They would imagine she had intentionally followed them. That she was spying. Inching one foot back, then the other, she parted the shrubs, without regard for the branches that stung her arms and face as they snapped back into place. As she transferred her weight onto her other foot, the ground slid away beneath her, and she stepped into an oozing ditch. Her ankle turned as she fell, and she landed sprawling with one foot twisted under her. The pain was so sharp and unexpected, she wasn't able to prevent an outcry of anguish.

"What in the world was that?"

"We'll soon find out."

CHAPTER SIX

AFRAID TO MOVE, Melissa huddled in the shadows, clutching her injured ankle, hoping it wasn't sprained and praying that she wouldn't be discovered.

"Are you mad?" Natalie screeched. "Don't go over there. Have one of the servants investigate. Who knows what maniac could be lurking in those bushes?"

"Whoever it is, we'll handle it."

Melissa pressed herself deeper into the shrubbery as the voices came closer. But it was futile. Jeremy located her in seconds.

"What the hell are you doing back there?" he thundered, his face looming toward her. "I've— Melissa? Is that you?"

"I don't believe this," Natalie wailed, coming up behind him. "It's that pesky girl again."

"Are you all right?" Jeremy dropped to one knee on the grass beside her. "Can you move your leg?"

Melissa tried tentatively, then moaned a negative reply.

"Miss Brandon, get up," Natalie ordered her.

"She could be seriously hurt. My damned gardener didn't fill in the hole when he took out that diseased elm. He was in such a bloody hurry to get through."

"How could he possibly know someone would be skulking around back here? What's the matter, Miss Brandon, couldn't you find a dancing partner?"

"That's enough, Natalie." Jeremy touched a hand to the injured foot. "I'll have to get you into the house, Melissa. Slide your arm around my neck. Easy now. A little at a time. That's it."

"You don't mean to carry her! She's head to foot with mud. She'll ruin your jacket."

"To hell with my jacket. Okay, little one. Relax. I've got you."

"I can walk," Melissa said helplessly, as he scooped her into his arms. "I just need a minute until—"

"Didn't you hear her?" Natalie asked. "She wants to walk."

"For the last time," Jeremy snarled, "will you shut up?"

"Not in there," Melissa pleaded, as Jeremy started toward the house and the crowded ballroom. "I don't want to spoil things for—for Jean."

"I'll take you through the library. Don't worry. No one will see us."

"No. By all means, don't worry your pretty little head!" Natalie snorted, flouncing off in the other direction.

"I'm terribly sorry," Melissa murmured.

"I'm the one who should apologize. That hole had no business being there." Inside the library, Jeremy set her carefully on the couch and eased off first one shoe, then the other. "There's a doctor here somewhere," he said. "I'll have him take a look at you. Then I'll see you home."

"You can't do that." She could imagine Natalie's reaction to his playing chauffeur and missing his own party. There would be a king-sized war she wasn't fit to wage. "I'd crawl first."

He flicked on a table lamp and stood back, raking his fingers through his hair. It was disheveled and fell over his forehead now, as it had the first time she saw him. Frustrated, he made a clicking sound with his tongue. "You aren't used to anybody telling you what to do, are you?"

Now that the pain had dulled to an ache and she was better able to consider what had happened, she felt like such an idiot, she couldn't stop the tears from welling in her eyes. "I'm not trying to be argumentative. I appreciate what you're doing. It's just that..." How could she explain, when she wasn't free to tell the truth? "It's just that this hasn't been the best vacation I've ever had. Tonight was—"

"None of that now." He tore off his jacket and let it fall over the back of a chair. Then he loosened his tie, pulled a footstool close and sat down. The dim light from the lamp cast deep shadows on his face, accentuating its bone structure. "Your holiday isn't over yet, little one. It can still be salvaged. And I have a hunch that from here on, it's going to be all you hoped it would be."

He leaned forward, putting his weight partly on the couch, and she noticed to her embarrassment that there was an ugly streak of mud on his shirtfront. His pants were muddy, as well. He couldn't possibly join the party again without changing.

"Your clothes," she cried.

"Nothing a trip to the cleaners won't cure. I don't believe the prognosis for your dress is so good, though."

She regarded the wrinkled and torn dress that had once been a gown she'd coveted, then scrimped and saved to own. Her heart sank like a stone.

"I'll buy you another," he offered, reading her thoughts.

"You won't. It was my own foolishness that caused this." She adjusted the ripped place in her skirt that exposed far more leg than she'd realized and winced in pain at the sudden movement.

He frowned. "Let me have a look at that ankle." Pressing here and there, he examined her foot, turning it from one side to the other. "Nothing appears to be broken, but I'm not a doctor. It should be X-rayed."

"If it isn't better tomorrow, I'll see to it."

"Damn right you will. I'll pick you up and take you to a doctor myself in the morning."

"No!" she said with more vehemence than she'd intended.

He closed one eye. "Don't you ever say anything but no?"

"Really, it'll be all right. My ankle's been twisted much worse than this before."

"I'm not surprised, if you make a practice of creeping around beach houses and dark gardens at night. Tell me, what were you doing out there?"

In the excitement, she'd all but forgotten the intimate scene she'd stumbled upon: Jeremy and Natalie huddled together in the shadows. Now it was fresh in her mind again, and she wondered if he was attempting to learn how much she'd seen and heard.

"Maybe I'm a cat woman," she said, with equal parts humor and sarcasm. "Cursed by generations of other cat people to prowl at night, hunting down my victims."

"Maybe you are at that," he said, falling in with her nonsense. "Now that you mention it, there is something definitely feline about you. It's in the tilt of your eyes, in your walk, and most of all, in the way you strike without warning.''

"I'm shamefully lacking in feline grace, though," she said, apologetically.

"Should I be afraid of you?" He moved his tongue slowly across his upper lip. "Can I be transformed, too, by your touch?"

"Maybe."

"By your kiss?" The question was all but whispered.

"I wanted some fresh air." She wriggled to set her back more comfortably against the smoothness of the leather couch and to put more distance between them. "It's a beautiful night and I felt like walking. There isn't anything mysterious or sinister about it."

"Why are you always so defensive?"

"I'm not—always."

"Then I make you feel the need to defend yourself?"

She considered his question and decided to give it an honest answer. "Yes, you do."

"Mmm. I see. Why is that?"

It was a demand for an answer, rather than a request. When she shifted her weight, he shifted his, as well, and was now closer than ever. His nearness was disconcerting. It wouldn't allow her to give voice to her thoughts or to sort them out with any clarity.

Besides, he already knew why. He only wanted the satisfaction of hearing her say it. This room was more suitable to her original picture of him, she thought, than was the rest of the house. The walls that weren't lined with books were gleaming dark wood panels, and the furniture was polished oak and leather.

Without his jacket and in these less-pretentious sur-roundings he was almost the man she had met in Eli's shack. If only he could have been that man. If only there hadn't been Natalie Kerr and the ridiculous need to masquerade.

If only...

She gasped as he touched a hand to her face when she hadn't expected it. Never had she been so hyperrecep-tive, so alive with sensation—so aware of scents, of textures and sounds. Jeremy's hand was rough. His palm was calloused, though she wouldn't have expected it.

"Tell me why, Melissa," he said, in a voice that reached deep inside her being, to touch something that had never been touched before.

She was a challenge to him, she reminded herself with a new desperation, trying to still the throbbing within her, before he felt it, too. Before he noticed the high color in her cheeks and caught the telltale moisture that was forming on her forehead. She'd stood up to him, and that was intolerable after the treatment he was used to getting.

Remember how changeable he is? Remember how he glared at you from the ledge? Remember how close he was to Natalie in the garden? Remember? Remember?

"Tell me, Melissa," he repeated, making her name sound as it had never sounded on anyone's lips before.

She had to search her mind to make sense of the question. "Because—because you always seem to be thinking so much more than you say."

"You're very perceptive."

"Why don't you come out and say what you mean, then?" It was a feeble attempt to put everything back into perspective. To make him angry, if necessary, so that the danger could pass.

"Why don't I?" He moved from the footstool to the couch. The hard muscles of his thigh tensed against her, and the hand that had come to rest on her shoulder found its way to her back to support her and bring her nearer him. The room was warm, and the scent of him rose to her nostrils. "You want me to be more direct?"

"Yes. No. I mean—yes." Her lips parted in anticipation of the kiss she'd thought about almost from the beginning. She could stop it, she knew. His was a fragile ego, though he tried to pretend otherwise. The wrong gesture, a sharp word, and the elemental battle she waged within herself would be won. Or would it?

A tremor passed through her, and she released a pent-up breath, hoping he hadn't noticed. Then she realized that the tremor had been his. She had only been touched by its vibration. "You've ignited a spark inside me, little one," he said. "A spark I was sure had gone out long ago. But it isn't acceptable, is it, to tell a woman you've only just met that you want more than anything to make love to her? Aren't there formalities in the modern world? Rituals civilized society demands first?"

"Are there?" she asked, not recognizing her own voice.

"Aren't there?"

This is it. The point of no return. His face flamed against hers and, spellbound, she waited for what seemed an eternity as his mouth—his wonderful mouth—opened slowly and enclosed hers in a paralyzing kiss that fulfilled all its promises and offered more. Was it only one kiss?

He didn't raise his lips from hers, even when hers quivered and moved in response. Even when her tongue darted against his to meet its caress. But it felt as if it were two, three, four kisses—more—all swept into one ever-deepening one that raised havoc inside her. Had there been an explosion, she wouldn't have noticed it. She would have only supposed it had taken place in her own heart.

When, with reluctance, he allowed his lips to leave hers, they stayed no more than an inch away, tantalizing her. "I'll get you home," he said. "You should get out of that dress."

"Yes, I should," she agreed brokenly.

He eased himself away, smoothing her arm, touching her hand and, at last, her fingertips until he stood. "I want to know everything about you, little one," he said. "Everything that makes you the person you are."

"I don't think you'll find anything very extraordinary."

"I already have. Come on." He reached for her. "Up you go."

"You needn't carry me now. I can walk."

He curled his hand into a fist and shook it at her. "Try it, and see what happens."

"But—"

Scooping her easily into his arms, he silenced her protest with a greedy kiss that set the core of her womanhood ablaze.

"Your party..."

"I won't be missed. Besides, there are more important considerations."

"Such as?" She wound her arms around his neck and smiled dreamily, his strength making her feel weightless.

"Such as..."

"SHE'S IN HERE," Natalie screeched, sweeping through the door, with Brian close behind her.

Brian filled the doorway, and judging by the jut of his jaw and the florid color in his face, his mood hadn't improved. It had been reinforced by a few tips of the bottle. He might have been a wrongfully used husband for the fury that lit his eyes. "What the hell is this?"

"I'm going to drive Melissa home," Jeremy explained. "She shouldn't be walking on this ankle until we have it looked at by someone who knows what he's doing."

"Isn't that stretching the responsibility of a host too far, York?" Brian's voice was a sneer.

"Really, Jeremy!" Natalie added her protest.

"They're right," Melissa said, coming to herself again. She wriggled against Jeremy's hold on her. How could she even have considered allowing him to desert his guests on her account? Besides, after everything that had passed between them she needed time alone to think. "I'll be fine. Put me down. Please."

"I'll take her," Brian growled, stepping in. "After all, I brought her here. I think I'm capable of taking her home."

Jeremy's eyes struck Melissa's with a look that somehow implied betrayal. "Of course," he said stiffly.

Before she could say anything more, she was deposited in Brian's arms as if she were a package being returned to sender.

Brian jerked his head toward the outside doors. "Can we leave this way?"

"Follow the path to your left. It's dark, so watch your step. I'll have someone bring your car around."

"Brian, dear," Natalie cooed. "I would use a bit of restraint and not, ah, bother Melissa tonight. She needs her rest. Be sure and tuck her in nice and snug, though. The poor little thing is always tripping over her own feet.''

"Aren't you coming?'' he wanted to know.

"Gracious, no. Don't worry about Jean and me. We'll get a ride home.'' She flashed Jeremy one of her most brilliant smiles and slipped an arm through his. "From someone.''

CHAPTER SEVEN

BEFORE MELISSA COULD STOP BRISTLING inside over what had happened, they were home, and Brian had set a kettle on to boil. "Why did Natalie try so hard to make Jeremy believe there's something between you and me?" she demanded. "And why did you let her do it?"

"I didn't expect you to fall for York's phony brand of charm."

"What makes you think I've fallen for anything?"

"Haven't you?"

"I don't know."

He slammed a hand against the wall. "That's what I mean."

"I'm only trying to be honest." She settled on the couch, stretching her sore leg out to rest it, and closed her eyes. While she was being honest with Brian, she might as well be honest with herself.

After tonight she wouldn't even try to shrug off the overpowering physical attraction she felt for Jeremy. It was numbing and complete and would probably only grow stronger, given the chance. But no matter what Brian told her to the contrary, she was confident, for a time at least, that Jeremy had been sincere. There had been a few shining moments when their souls had touched. Those moments had been independent of what might have been termed as "chemistry."

"Would you like me to pour you a bath?" Brian asked, somewhat subdued.

The cuckoo clock sounded, and she waited until the little wooden bird was silent before answering. Brian hadn't meant to hurt her. What good would there be in punishing him now?

"That would be nice," she managed, trying to erase from her mind's eye the picture of Jeremy's face when Natalie had told Brian to "tuck her in nice and snug."

"I like the water scalding."

Obviously relieved, Brian knelt beside the couch. "Listen, York will hurt you if you let him. Do you think he would have behaved differently if his wife were alive?"

"What are you suggesting?"

"I told you he and Natalie were once in love. That he left her to marry Kathryn Havelock."

"That was years ago."

"But I didn't tell you that his marriage didn't end his affair with Natalie. When she came here for a visit, it was on again. They met, discreetly of course, whenever the opportunity presented itself."

"I don't believe you. You obviously detest Jeremy, and I get the feeling you'd say anything to turn me against him."

"To the Yorks, people like you, me and Nat are to be tolerated, used and thrown away," he went on, too wound up by the events of the evening to listen to Melissa's objections. "We're commoners. Our feelings don't count."

"There's a big hole in your theory," she interrupted. "Natalie shouldn't be included on your list. Her marriage made her a wealthy woman, didn't it?"

He snorted. "You don't understand these people at all, do you, kitten? With the Yorks and their kind, money is important, but it takes second place. They have disdain for the newly rich. The 'parvenu,' as they call them. A woman like Nat who marries wealth, or Mr. X who manages to accumulate it with sweat, tears and a lot of luck is an upstart. A pretender. A person has to be at least third generation to have social standing and be accepted in the circle of blue bloods."

Melissa was suddenly too tired to argue with him. "Could you pour that bath now?" she asked with a weary sigh.

"I'm sorry if it hurts you to hear this," Brian said, somewhat calmer now. "But do you seriously believe Natalie was the only one York played around with all those years? Or for that matter, that you were the only woman he held in his arms tonight?"

She wouldn't listen to him anymore. It hurt too much. She'd close out his voice as she had done when she was a child and an adult scolded too much. Shutting her eyes, she tried to imagine herself sinking deeper and deeper into the cushions.

Undoubtedly Brian realized he had gone too far. He stopped talking at once. Then she heard him start up the stairs to fix her tub.

After her bath, sleep didn't come at once, but when it did, mercifully, it lasted through the night. In the morning she woke with a start when she heard someone tiptoeing beside her bed.

"Oh Missy, did I wake you?" Her sister clasped her hands together and brought them to her mouth. "They told me what happened. How's your poor foot?"

"It's still there."

The girl flopped on the bed, just missing Melissa's sore ankle, tucked her legs under her and began humming tunelessly. "There's trouble brewing. Natalie thinks you did what you did on purpose."

"That isn't headline news."

"She's mad at me, too."

"Why? Did you take a minute and a quarter to play the 'Minute Waltz'?"

"Nothing so catastrophic. No. It's Todd. She wants me to stay away from him. She thinks I'll slip up and spill her game plan."

Melissa threw back the covers and eased herself up gingerly. She could walk, though it might be wise to get some bandages and bind her foot for support. Then, Natalie or no, it was down to the kitchen for something to eat. She was starving. With all the lovely food at the party, she hadn't had a bite.

"Don't you think Natalie has a valid point?" she asked her sister. "What if you really got to like Todd? With you posing as Jean, where would you be?"

"Exactly where I am now." Arlene heaved a sigh that came from the soles of her feet. "I already like him more than I've ever liked anybody. He's, well, I can't explain how he makes me feel."

There was a sharp knock at the door. "Jean, are you in there?" It was Natalie.

"Yes, I am." Arlene crossed her eyes and stuck out her tongue.

"Don't dawdle if you want to go to practice. I've umpteen things to do."

"Practice?" Melissa asked after Natalie had moved away from the door.

"The custodian at the auditorium is going to unlock the doors for me so I can practice on that piano for my performance at the big doings Friday night."

"That's nice of him."

"Very nice. Except that I'm not going to practice. That's why I came in here to see you."

"Why do I have the feeling that I should sit down again before I hear this?"

"I want a simple favor."

Todd, she explained, was coming at eleven. As far as Natalie was concerned, he would be taking Melissa for a drive. Arlene would allow Natalie to drive her to the auditorium. She'd pretend to go in. But when Natalie's car was out of sight, quick as a rabbit, she'd go to where Todd and Melissa would be waiting—after she explained to the custodian that there'd been a change in plans.

"Think again, baby."

"You can't mean you won't do it for me."

"I can, and I do."

"You're afraid of Natalie." The girl's voice was sullen.

"You know better than that. She couldn't despise me more than she does already."

"Then do it for me."

"I can't."

Arlene sprang off the bed and faced her, and Melissa felt a stab of regret. Even in her pink, shorty nightgown, her sister suddenly looked like a woman. Were people right when they accused her of hating to see her grow up?

"I've always told you everything," Arlene said, "and I'm telling you that Todd means a lot to me. I'm also telling you that I have plans. I wouldn't throw away my talent—yes, I know I have talent—by marrying foolishly. For that matter, Todd has something besides sawdust in his head. We only want to be together. I'd hate myself forever if I turned my back on him."

And you'd hate me, too, Melissa added silently. "Where do you plan to go?" she asked.

"To Mystic. It's a little seafaring village not far from here. Todd says it's straight out of the history books. There's a mariner's museum there and scads of old ships."

"And suddenly you're crazy about ships? What am I supposed to do with myself all day?"

"Take a sketch pad. You could draw some fantastic sea gull pictures."

"Sea gulls. For how many hours?"

"I'd do it for you. Oh, don't you see? Everyone's against Todd and me."

"By everybody, you mean Natalie."

"And her pompous pal, Jeremy. Last night she sent me back here with some friends of hers that were coming this way. I forget what inane excuse she gave for staying at the party. She'd be right home, she said. Hah! I heard Jeremy and her drive up at about four-thirty this morning. They sat in his car for another hour after that. I can't understand how she dragged herself out of bed this early."

Melissa shook the glass paperweight and tried to sound offhand as she watched the snow swirl down on the tiny cottage below. "What makes you think Todd's brother is against you?"

"By the way he looks at me. The way he interrogates me. Honestly, he makes me feel as if I'm applying for membership in some exclusive country club or something. And I heard him make Natalie promise to keep Todd and me apart.''

"Are you sure?''

"He said he didn't want us spending any more time together. Todd might lose his head over me, he told her. Then *he'd* have to step in.''

Purposefully, Melissa set the paperweight down before she was tempted to throw it. Had Brian spoken the truth about Jeremy's irrational prejudices? Did Jeremy actually believe that her sister's pedigree—or Natalie's daughter's for that matter—wasn't good enough to allow her to associate with a York? "We'd better not waste any more time, if we're going to pull this off," she said. "What will I wear?''

"I already took your white pants out and pressed your blue-and-white-striped shirt. Just the right outfit for your strolling-young-artist look. Oh, your foot's all right, isn't it? You can stroll.''

Melissa had to laugh. "Yes. My foot's much better. You were pretty certain I'd agree, weren't you?''

With her sister's help, she'd just managed to get dressed when Todd drove up.

Natalie, who'd heard the car door slam, sprang to the window as the girls came downstairs. "What is *he* doing here? I told Jean in no uncertain terms—''

"He's here for me," Melissa said.

The woman's jaw sagged. "If you can't get one York, you'll try for another. Is that it?''

Pretending not to hear, Melissa threw open the door just as Todd raised a hand to knock. "Ready to go, Melissa?''

"All ready.''

"Don't worry, Mrs. Kerr," Todd said solicitously. "I'll take real good care of her.''

Her sister had obviously filled him in on Natalie's explosive temper. It was all he could do to contain his mirth as they turned, arm in arm, and started down the steps. "Did Jean tell you how grateful we are that you're doing this?" he asked when they were out of earshot.

"She told me." Melissa found it too disconcerting to look at him squarely. There was entirely too much Jeremy in his face for her to feel comfortable. Except that he wasn't Jeremy. Todd was down-to-earth and sincere.

Or maybe all the Yorks had inherited acting ability along with their fortunes.

"We'll have breakfast if you want," he suggested, pulling up in front of the Sea View, the rendezvous point.

"I want. Everything happened so fast, I didn't have a chance to eat."

Over tea and toast, he spoke of Arlene—Jean—with affection and talked of his plans for earning a place in the family company. He didn't want anything handed to him on a silver platter.

"I won't say it hasn't made things a heck of a lot easier being an heir. I probably wouldn't have gotten anybody to listen to me if I weren't a York. But when they listen, I plan to have something worthwhile to say."

He was in the middle of a story about a boyish prank he'd once played on his older brother, when suddenly he tapped Melissa's hand and looked past her, glassy-eyed. "Oh, oh. Speak of the devil."

Melissa turned her head to see Jeremy approaching. He didn't look at all surprised to see her, and why should he? Natalie would have snatched up the phone and given him the latest news flash before their car had pulled away from the curb. He had charged over in his trusty Mercedes to rescue his baby brother from the clutches of Mata Hari.

"I noticed your car in front," he said to Todd, though his eyes speared Melissa. If he was attempting to sound light-hearted he missed the mark by more than a tad. "I thought you were supposed to be at a business meeting about the Emmet property."

"Not until next week." Todd twisted his mouth to one side. "You know that. You set the meeting up."

Jeremy snapped his fingers. "I forgot."

"You forgot? That's hard to believe." He shook his head as if to gather his wits. "Melissa and I are planning to run over to Mystic. I thought I'd show her the museum."

"I didn't expect to see you up and about this morning, Melissa. Your ankle," Jeremy said pointedly, as though she needed a reminder.

"I told you it was nothing."

"So you did."

"Excuse me, you two." Todd touched a foot against one of Melissa's under the table. He would probably try to head her sister off and keep her hidden until Jeremy had gone. "I'll be right back."

Jeremy nodded and squeezed into his brother's place in the booth. He summoned the waitress, ordered a cup of coffee and sat looking out the window toward the sea as he drank it. If theirs was a waiting game, he was prepared to play it. "Your friend does have a time keeping track of you, doesn't he?" he said, after the silence had been long enough for both of them to feel it.

So now his anger would be turned on her, Melissa thought. Well, she wouldn't allow it to trouble her. When she'd started at the insurance company, she'd been a relief switchboard operator and had been railed at regularly by irate customers for everything from their being denied claims to the cost of their coverage. She could handle anything Jeremy dished out, as long as it helped to take the pressure off her sister.

"I do what I like," she said. "I don't have to account to anyone."

"So I notice." His smile bordered on a grimace. "Doesn't it get somewhat difficult at times, keeping your admirers apart?"

She smiled, too. It was good to see the oh, so-cool Mr. York hot under the collar. "I have a good filing system."

"Do you know what you're doing?" He spoke through tight lips. His expression didn't change, but the small vein at his temple pulsated.

"Of course, I'm planning to enjoy what's left of my holiday."

"At any cost. And how does Todd figure into those plans?"

"Are you asking my intentions?" A teasing laugh hid the tremor in her voice. It wasn't as easy to continue the verbal sparring as she'd supposed it would be. Why didn't he just go away and leave her alone?

"It might be more fitting to ask about the intentions of Brian Hendricks and what claim he has on you."

"How does that concern you?"

"I didn't imagine the way you kissed me last night."

"The way I kissed *you*?"

"Will Todd be caught in the middle of whatever game it is you're playing?"

"Todd isn't a child."

His hand snaked out, and his fingers closed around her wrist. But before he could say whatever he'd planned to say, he was distracted by the sight of her sister, shoes in hand, running toward the Sea View. Todd hadn't managed to intercept her in time, Melissa realized. She'd arrived on the beach side, while Todd had been watching for her on the road.

Yanking free of Jeremy's grasp with a sudden twist, Melissa watched helplessly. Todd spotted Arlene, and the two moved together, whispering and sneaking surreptitious glances toward the restaurant. If it had been a silent movie, there would have been no need for subtitles to allow Jeremy to figure out their scheme. Melissa didn't need them either to read Jeremy's thoughts as he looked at her again.

"And then there were four," he muttered, his maddening half smile returning.

"Jean decided it was too nice a day to stay cooped inside at the keyboard," Todd explained when they reached the booth. "She's coming to Mystic with us."

"Good idea." Jeremy motioned for the check. "If you don't mind, I'll tag along, too."

More silent-movie glances were exchanged as he signed for breakfast, pretending not to notice the confusion he'd caused.

Finally Todd managed to emit an over-enthusiastic, "Great! The more the merrier."

"We'll take my car," Jeremy offered on the way to the parking lot. "There's more room."

"If you want," Todd replied. Then with sudden inspiration added, "It'll be better for you to ride in front with Jer, Melissa—so your foot won't be cramped. Amanda and I will take the back."

Jeremy opened the car door and waited while the two climbed in. Then he reached out to help Melissa. A stony glare was her answer to him, as she rubbed her wrist to remind him of how his fingers had dug into her flesh.

"I can manage," she told him under her breath.

"You won't tell mother about this, will you, Jeremy?" her sister asked in her plaintive wanting-a-favor voice. "She thinks I'm practicing."

"No," he assured her. "We all need a break from routine now and then."

Oh no, Melissa thought to herself, trying to wilt him with a look that telegraphed her doubt. He wouldn't say a word. Not until he could get to a phone.

As the car sped along the highway, the conspirators in the back seat spoke in voices too soft to be heard. Jeremy said nothing. Likely he was attempting to catch telltale parts of their conversation. Melissa was more than content to sit quietly and watch the scenery whiz past. She would, she decided, enjoy the outing in spite of her unwelcome companion.

CHAPTER EIGHT

ALONG THE COBBLED STREETS of Mystic sat shops from another time, where present-day craftsmen went about their work as if no progress had taken place in the rest of the world. Here were coopers with their barrels and casks, chandlers and apothecaries, as well as sail makers. At the General Store, Arlene was taken with the glass jars of old-fashioned stick candy and insisted on treating each of them.

After touring the museum, an old school house and a tavern, they went through a building where miniature ships were displayed. An enthusiast for things of the sea, Todd was eager to get back to the docks to give an old whaling ship a more thorough inspection.

"How's your ankle?" he asked Melissa. "You seem to be favoring your other foot."

"Yes, you shouldn't be doing so much walking," her sister hastened to add.

It sounded to Melissa as though they were reciting lines they'd written together. "I'm fine," she argued. "I think the walking has actually made me feel better."

"I don't see how it could," Todd said.

"If you aren't careful you might have to spend the rest of your holiday on crutches." Arlene turned her back to Jeremy and twisted her face into a comical expression of pleading. It meant that Melissa was expected to cooperate with their transparent plan.

"Why don't I take Jean back to the ships?" Todd proposed, as if the thought had only just occurred to him. "You and Jer can take the car and see whatever you want to see. Then we'll meet later."

"I don't need a babysitter."

"That's open to debate," Jeremy muttered.

"Jer's been here so many times, he wouldn't mind doing it that way. In fact, he'd probably rather. Right, Jer? You two can find a good place to eat lunch. I know you're famished."

"You haven't eaten anything much, either," Melissa tried.

"We'll grab something on the run."

"No one has to stay with me. I can rest on the benches if I feel the need. There's plenty of shade and—"

"Synchronize," Todd broke in, holding a wrist up for his brother to see his watch. "We'll meet in this spot in two hours."

"One hour," Jeremy corrected.

"An hour and a half."

Jeremy looked away in resignation. "Not a minute more."

"I would think I'd have something to say about the arrangements," Melissa protested as the other couple hurried away together.

"I'm not any more pleased about this than you are," Jeremy told her, with his usual show of chivalry.

"I didn't ask for your company. Go on. If you hurry you can still catch up."

"And leave you here? You know Todd wouldn't go for that. If you'd stayed home as you should have, this wouldn't have happened. None of this would have happened. As it is, you're stuck with me, and you deserve it." He rubbed his hands together briskly, as if he felt his insulting little speech had cleared the air. "Now. Anything more on foot is out of the question. I suggest we pick up some lunch and drive somewhere to enjoy it."

She shrugged. Where they went would make little difference. She'd never been in a car with a sunroof before. It gave all the cooling pleasure of a convertible, without the drawback of a driving wind to send long hair flying every which way, tangling it and obscuring vision. With boxed fried chicken, hard rolls and a carton of fresh-squeezed orange juice tucked into a carton on the back seat, they were on their way.

It would have suited Melissa had they kept driving, on and on, in silence. But before long they saw a sign advising them there was a picnic area ahead, and Jeremy turned off.

"The tables are taken," she told him. "It's a beautiful day. We aren't the only ones to have noticed this place."

"Picnic tables are hard and uncomfortable, anyway," he said. "And usually covered with ants."

"Then—"

"Wouldn't you rather be adventurous and find a spot away from the roar of the highway?"

"We don't have a tablecloth."

"I have something that'll serve." He opened the car trunk, pulled out a blanket and gave it a shake or two.

Melissa raised an eyebrow. "Always prepared?"

He thrust the blanket at her. "You take this. I'll carry the lunch."

"The ants won't be able to find us back here?" she asked, trying to keep up with him as he wound his way through the trees.

"Only the discerning ones."

"Do you often take impulse outings like this one?"

"No," he said. "I enjoy my work. More than I do most outings."

She wasn't surprised to hear it. "Do you have an office in town?"

"No. I work out of the house most of the time, though there isn't much being accomplished this week, I'm afraid, with all the chaos caused by the bicentennial. You might say I'm on an enforced holiday."

"I can't help but wonder what led you to do what you do," she said. "I understand that designing amusement park rides wasn't the family business. But a branch-off of your own."

His eyes were steely gray in the muted sunlight. "Why did you go into insurance? Was your father an insurance man and his father before him?"

"Actually, I have no interest in your reasons," she snapped back at him. "I thought we should make an attempt at conversation, since, as you so courteously put it, we'll be stuck with each other for a while."

"I'm sorry." He slapped his free hand to the back of his neck. "I'm not at my best today."

Or any other day, she added silently, still bristling. "Forget it."

"I had a cousin," he said, ducking under a low-hanging branch, then holding it up to allow her through. "He was the black sheep of the family because he ran off and joined a carnival show. I wasn't permitted to make contact with him, but I did. Through an aunt, his mother. Whenever his show came within driving distance, he'd collect me and take me back with him. We'd ride everything from one end of the midway to the other. Then we'd start all over again. He had a head full of ideas for new, unheard-of attractions. He'd sketch them for me on paper and talk endlessly about the time when he'd have enough money saved so that he could get a show of his own together. He always said I'd be his partner."

"Is he with you now?"

"All his ideas stayed on paper, unfortunately. He never had more than a dollar or two in his pockets. One night his rig went of control on the highway, and he was killed."

"How terrible."

"It happened a long time ago. I would guess his enthusiasm sparked an enthusiasm in me that stuck."

"And so you did it for him."

"You could say that. Partly. Some of my ideas are based on his original sketches. He had a remarkable imagination. If only the family could have provided him with some backing." He stopped and looked around. "Is this spot okay?"

"I think there's a brook nearby. I hear running water."

"A little farther then," he agreed. "What about you? Why did you choose insurance?"

"Math was always my best subject in school. I used to solve complicated problems just for the fun of doing them. But I wouldn't say insurance was a burning ambition. Until I was twelve, I wanted to be a deep-sea diver. I wanted to be the one who brought up the Titanic."

He laughed. "Single-handed?"

"Naturally."

"There's your brook," he said, and they stood for a moment looking at the poor trickle of gurgling water. "Not exactly Niagara Falls."

"It'll do. Where's your imagination?"

"Under control, for the moment," he told her. "Fortunately." When she gave him a questioning look, he added, "A man's imagination can get him into hot water."

And a woman's, she agreed inside herself, thinking how easily she could let herself fall under Jeremy's spell. Whenever she was with him, she felt on the brink of something. Whether that something meant disaster or bliss, she didn't know.

After they'd spread their blanket, the lunch box was set to one side and forgotten for the moment as they silently settled down to appreciate their chosen spot.

It was unexpected to discover a tiny woodland so close to civilization. Here, in a tangle of moss, yellow clover and thistle, grew wildflowers in shades of purple and gold. A brown squirrel near the water's edge spied them and scurried for cover. What other little creatures lay in hiding, watching them? Melissa wondered. Across the brook grew a strangely gnarled and twisted thorn-bush, like those pictured in children's books—those that hid the "wee folk" until they could safely creep out at night and join the fairy ring. Maybe those fairies and elves were even able to work their magic from their hiding places, she mused. A feeling of contentment had swept over her since she and Jeremy had come upon this spot. Certainly that feeling had reached him, too. He looked relaxed and more like the Jeremy who'd touched her heart.

When he was deep in thought she could see the child in him. The child who could unreservedly thrill over a bustling fairground or the reaction of a midway crowd to a simple carnival ride.

"Have you known Jean long?" he asked.

She would have loved to paint him as he looked now. Though sometimes she questioned her ability to transfer exactly the look she wanted from her mind's eye to the canvas, this time she felt inspired. Certainly she could paint his eyes—eyes that were deep and luminous and full of mystery.

He was staring at her now. "Have you?" he asked again, and she realized that her mind had wandered too far from the here and now.

"Have I what?"

"I asked you if you'd known Natalie's daughter long. Have you?" His patience seemed to be clinging to only a thread as he waited.

"Yes," she answered, deciding not to volunteer one extra syllable of information.

Sensitive eyes or no, his technique was about as subtle as that of a pie-in-the-face, baggy-pants comic. It was crystal clear now why he had allowed the two couples to separate. He figured there was comparative safety in the tourist bustle of Mystic. If he got Melissa alone, he could wheedle answers out of her. Hence the picnic with Mother Nature's backdrop.

Think again, Mr. York.

"Is she really as sweet and unspoiled as she appears to be?"

"She is. Tell me, is Todd as unaffected as he pretends?"

His eyebrows drew a fraction closer together in preparation for a scowl. He caught onto her game quickly. Each question he asked about her sister, she answered in monosyllables and countered with a similar one about Todd.

"Is it true that music is the most important thing in her life? Or is it Natalie's ambition that drives her?"

"Haven't you heard her play?"

"No, but I'm told she's very good," he conceded.

"Good? She's more than just good. What about Todd? Does he truly like the family business, or is it something he's gone into because it's expected of him?"

Jeremy sucked in his breath, scooped up a handful of stones and one by one tossed them into the stream. He didn't seem angry, though. "You're being defensive again."

"With good reason."

"Oh?"

"You can stop fretting about your brother," Melissa said, suddenly cutting to the heart of the matter. "She's fond of Todd, but she isn't contemplating anything rash."

"You're sure of that?"

"She may be young, but she has common sense enough to know that summertime romances usually don't work." Especially when everyone is against it, she might have added—but didn't, in deference to keeping the peace.

A single ray of lemon-colored sunlight fought its way through the leafy spread of branches overhead to shine in Melissa's eyes. She shifted her weight to avoid its glare. At the same instant, Jeremy leaned back on his elbow. The action brought him precariously close.

"What has common sense got to do with being in love?" he grunted, his lower lip jutting forward slightly.

It would have been too obvious to move away, so she didn't. But her own lips felt swollen and feverish. She didn't dare to lick them for fear he might suspect the effect his nearness was having on her. It was warm. Too warm. "If a woman keeps her wits about her," she went on, "she can recognize danger in a relationship before it becomes a danger. She can stop before it reaches that crucial point."

"Can she?"

She wanted so badly to be kissed. She actually felt the physical need to be kissed. And it was growing stronger. *Can she? Can she?* His question vibrated through her mind over and over until it became her own question— until it had lost its meaning. She couldn't remember what she'd been saying.

"And if she doesn't want to stop?" he persisted.

"Stop?"

He smiled and fastened his attention on her mouth. "You said..."

She swallowed hard as he touched the fragile silver chain she wore around her neck. It held a heart-shaped locket her father had given her for her fifteenth birthday. It still held the picture of the boy she had dated in high school.

"Does it open?"

"Yes, but—"

He pried the locket open, frowned at the picture inside, and closed it again without comment. "And you have this common sense you were talking about? You could put an end to a relationship you believed was threatening?"

She stared at the locket, searching her mind for something sensible to say. "I've never gotten around to changing the photograph. The opening is very small, you see, and I haven't wanted to cut a full-sized snapshot, just to get another face to put inside. If there were another face, that is."

He nodded gravely, as if she had uttered great words of wisdom.

Her flesh warmed at his touch. Ever-expanding circlets of pleasure rippled through her, as the pebbles Jeremy had tossed had made ripples on the water. Something—the soap he used, the shaving lotion, the shampoo—whatever it was, the subtle scent was will shattering.

"How did you do this?" His index finger traced the fine white scar over her left eyebrow.

She flinched as though he'd touched her with a hot poker. "I'd almost forgotten. How did you see it? It's so faint."

"It stands out when your face is flushed. How did it happen?"

So her face was flushed. "I fell out of an apple tree."

"I might have known. You climb trees, too?"

"Yes. That is, I used to."

"Poor little girl." He leaned toward her and pressed his lips to the spot. Without volition, her hand shot up to touch the place where his lips had been.

"I was trying to—"

Her train of thought stopped when he brought his mouth to her ear and his lips moved. Had she said something? She was too far over the edge to comprehend or even care about words.

The flutter of his breath communicated in its own way against her hypersensitive skin. It ripped away posturing and convention to reveal the true person shaped and molded by a lifetime of experience. It demanded naked acceptance. She wasn't ready for that— was she?

The guidelines she'd set up for her own behavior flashed on the periphery of her awareness and were discarded. She made fists of her hands, sensing a mutiny, and tried to keep them from playing at Jeremy's shoulders and chest to keep them from digging, finger by finger, into the taut muscled flesh of him, from reveling in the strength and power that was his.

No. She could still fight it. What had she been saying? She had to remember what she'd been saying. "I was trying to—to prove that I could climb as well as—"

"You're wrong." He cut her off almost angrily.

"I know that now. But I was never one to turn down a dare."

"I wasn't referring to your tree climbing."

"No?" A layer of cool air tickled her arms.

"No." Cupping a hand beneath her chin, he lifted it, tracing his thumb across her lower lip.

"What did you mean then?" She swallowed hard. "I was wrong?"

"I meant that common sense hasn't got a bloody thing to do with love."

Without conscious thought, she caught his hand and pressed it to her lips. His jaw slackened in surprise—though his surprise couldn't have been any stronger than her own. His eyes found hers and softened beautifully—magnificently—and she was treated to a glimpse of the Jeremy within. Their thoughts met, joined and grew stronger. He was remembering the taste of her, as she was remembering the taste of him. They were also sharing the same craving to enjoy the taste again.

This was the moment, she thought, and the wrestling began inside of her. No. Not here. Not now. Not with him.

"Oh hell," he groaned. "Do you know what you're doing?"

Yes, she answered without speaking. *Oh, yes.*

"This is madness," he said.

Yes. Sweet, sweet madness.

He rose, drawing her up with him, catching the blanket at the same time and, between feathery kisses, led her closer to the water.

"This is madness," he repeated, giving her another chance to protest, yet obviously aching for fear she might.

I know, she said again.

A mazelike path through thick-growing shrubbery brought them to a still-wilder spot, such as Rousseau might have created. Or did it only seem so because she was with Jeremy? They lay down again in the long shaggy grasses, and he moved over her.

"What's the use?" he muttered, catching her earlobe lightly between his lips. She found her voice and emitted a cry of pleasure, giving in to her desire to twist her fingers through the crisp tangle of his hair. How she'd longed to do it, almost from the first moment she'd seen him in Eli's cabin. Even later when she'd told herself she despised him.

A fusillade of kisses fell hotly on her forehead, her cheeks and down her neck. Luxuriating in an extended sigh, she allowed her head to fall back, wanting the feel of his mouth here—there—everywhere.

His eyes were glorious mirrors, reflecting her beauty as he saw it, reflecting a discovery that came only at those rare times when two people knew without reservation that their innermost longings were shared completely and honestly. Deliberately, he disciplined his ardor, wanting her to experience all that a woman can experience, lingering over the kiss her rushing senses demanded. Slowly, much too slowly, he dragged his lips back and forth across hers, then tasted with the tip of his tongue, allowing the sensation to fill them completely before imprisoning them.

They lay thigh to thigh, mouth to mouth, their hearts competing in hammering urgency, her body attempting to mold itself to his. And the marvelous certainty of his arousal filled her with joy.

With magnified senses she became aware of everything around them. She would remember the encouraging whisper of the trees, the gurgling of their own personal brook and the flutter of bird wings. She would recall later exactly how it felt when he caught up handfuls of the ebony hair, which spread like a pillow around her head. And how he'd buried his face in the freshly shampooed fragrance of it.

This delicious moment would be hers always, to cherish, to keep locked in her heart, to take out at times when she was alone and needed to know the wonder of him again.

She hardly noticed that he had unfastened her shirt, so deftly had he managed it, until it fell open. A fleeting thought struck her that he could only have done it if he were much practised. She forced the thought away. The past didn't matter. It wouldn't be allowed to intrude on their future.

One of his hands applied gentle pressure through the fabric of her bra and her breath caught in her throat. Someone could come along. She knew she should protest. Of course, she didn't. He might come to his senses and stop. Instead she voiced her quickening appetite with a moan of pleasure.

Freshly aroused, he slid a finger under the lacy edge, along the desire-scorched flesh, to discover the tight, rosy nipple. Then his hungry mouth set to work.

A SHRILL VOICE AND THEN ANOTHER invaded their special hidden place and allowed reality to rush in. Over the circle of greenery that hid them, children were calling to each other and laughing. "Hey! Neat-oh! Water. Let's take off our shoes."

"Civilization," Jeremy murmured and drew a shuddering breath as he held Melissa close briefly before moving away. "What am I going to do about you?"

Whatever you like, her heart sang as her fingers fumbled with her shirt buttons.

Five minutes more. If only she had five minutes more to savor her newfound contentment. The orderly side of her would have delighted in clearing away the clutter to make room in her memory for this shining moment. Wanting it to be safe, where she could recall it again easily and clearly, at will.

Her heart was full. But even as she accepted and cherished the precious gift of love she and Jeremy were able to give to each other now, one thing still bothered her. Where did Natalie fit into the picture?

Out of jealousy, Brian must have lied about the present relationship between his sister and Jeremy, and the past didn't matter. But Melissa herself had seen the two huddled in the garden, carrying on a conversation that sounded rather intimate.

And what about all the hours they'd spent together after the dance? Her sister had said they'd sat in the car until well after four o'clock in the morning. There had to be an explanation.

Of course, Jeremy would tell her in his own time. Ideally she should wait until he did. But to make the afternoon a perfect one for her, she had to know now.

It wouldn't be an easy subject to broach. She didn't want to sound like a possessive lover. It might even seem to Jeremy that she'd been spying on him.

"They'll be waiting for us," he said, looking at his watch.

Let them wait, was her first thought. They'd understand and applaud. This wasn't a moment to be easily discarded. "What about our lunch?" Melissa asked dreamily.

"Nibble as we go, if you're hungry," he said.

They arrived a little more than half an hour later than the time they'd agreed to meet, but there was no sign of the other couple. Jeremy behaved like a caged lion. He glared at his watch as if it were somehow responsible, checked it with the clock on the side of a building, stalked back and forth and glared at his watch again.

"They probably lost track of the time," Melissa suggested, wanting to soothe his agitation. "It's easy to do when you're having a good time." *Isn't it, Jeremy?* she added silently.

He shook his head and frowned. "It isn't like Todd. He's completely reliable."

The emphasis on *he* and *Todd* meant he blamed her sister for the lapse in his brother's reliability. "They'll be here. Why don't we sit on the bench and have something to eat? Maybe they arrived on schedule, saw we weren't here and went away again."

He turned on her. "What else do you see in your crystal ball?"

She blinked. Was this the same man who'd held her in his arms and kissed her only a short while ago? He was doing it again. Changing from Jekyll to Hyde. And it hurt.

"Mr. York? Are you Mr. York?" A pretzel vender was wheeling his cart toward them and calling out.

Jeremy whirled to face the man. "Yes?"

"Got a message for you, sir. Let me see." The man pushed back his cap and stared at the sky as though the message he had to deliver were written in the clouds.

"What is it?" From the expression on Jeremy's face, Melissa wouldn't have been surprised if he had grabbed the vender by the collar and shaken the message out of him.

"This young fella and his gal was here waiting for you. But a car full of their friends came along, they said, and they decided to ride on home with them. You shouldn't wait. I was supposed to tell you—you can take the car."

"Are you certain?"

The man cocked his head to one side and winked at Melissa playfully. "Would I lie to you? Do you want to buy a pretzel?"

"No!" Jeremy snarled.

"Nice and hot. Works up a healthy thirst for a cold beer."

"No, thank you," Melissa said quickly, hoping Jeremy wouldn't make a scene.

"Dammit!" He started toward the parking lot with Melissa hurrying as best she could to keep up with him.

"There's no reason to worry," she said. "I told you before—"

"You told me, did you?" he mocked. "You told me that your friend would have more sense. You've told me a great many things. Now tell me, when did you plan all this?"

"But I—"

"Obviously it was all arranged. Don't try and tell me otherwise. Your ankle conveniently bothered you because I got in the way. I had to stay behind and look after you."

"And I lured you off on that picnic."

"In a way. Yes."

"And I tried to take advantage of you." Tears stung her eyes, and she had to squeeze her hands against her sides to keep from slapping him.

"Congratulations. It worked." He threw the car door open. "Get in."

She took a step backward. "I don't intend to ride with you."

"Get in."

"I'll call someone to come for me."

"And if Hendricks isn't there, you'll hitchhike back to Sandgate?"

"I'd rather do that than suffer your insults."

With a muttered curse, he clamped his fingers painfully around her wrist as he had done at the restaurant. "You'll suffer more than my insults if you don't get in the car. Do I have to pick you up and throw you in?"

Trembling with fury, she teetered on the edge of indecision. Should she call his bluff? Surely he knew if he tried manhandling her in a public parking lot it might make the newspapers, as big as the York name was in these parts.

"You wouldn't dare."

"Is that your answer?"

"If I do get in," she told him, "it's only because I don't want to make Brian drive all the way here to get me."

"I don't give a damn for your reasons."

Their silence was grim this time, with Jeremy hunched over the steering wheel like a determined racing-car driver. Melissa reached for the knob of the radio, but he caught her hand and threw it back into her lap.

"I'm in no mood for music."

"I am."

"Then whistle."

It couldn't be happening, she told herself. But it was. A door had opened unexpectedly and allowed her a glimpse of the wonder that might have been. Then it had closed. The only logical explanation was that Jeremy had been pretending. The closeness she had felt in his arms was like a dream. His kiss, his touch, his murmured words of endearment had seemed beautiful. Now everything was sordid and ugly.

"My father left the decision making for the company with me," he said suddenly as if in answer to a question she'd asked. "I have a free rein."

"Good for you. But what are you talking about?"

"So if Jean believes that she'll be a wealthy woman if she marries Todd, she's mistaken. They can't marry. Perhaps you should tell her that."

"You tell her. Let her loathe you as I do."

As Jeremy screeched to a stop in front of the house, the curtains moved. The door flew open and Natalie, her hands pressed to her temples in what had become a characteristic pose, stood in the doorway watching. Melissa's sister stood behind her.

"So they didn't elope after all," Melissa snapped, infuriated by Jeremy's obvious relief. She let herself out of the car and slammed the door. "Your tantrum was all for nothing."

"Hold on a minute," he called, sprinting after her. "There's something that needs to be said."

"True. But my careful upbringing prevents me from saying it."

"Maybe you weren't part of a plan." He caught her arm and turned her toward him as she started up the stairs.

"Maybe I wasn't."

"If so, I apologize."

"If so? Your apology sounds like a business contract with its tacked-on qualifier. I find it unacceptable. Let me go."

"Melissa..."

She tried to shake herself loose from his grasp. "Take your despicable hands off me or I'll scream so loud every illustrious head will pop out of every royal window in your precious village."

"I wish with all my heart I hadn't allowed you to come with us. You don't even try to fit in," Natalie scolded as Melissa passed her. She touched a fluttery hand to Jeremy's shoulder, pantomiming her need for his strength in her hour of trial. "I'm sorry about all of this, dear. The girl constantly wheedles my daughter into doing things she would never do otherwise. She keeps everyone in an uproar, just to satisfy some twisted need she has for excitement."

Melissa might have screamed if she hadn't felt so drained. Her hurt foot throbbed, and every inch of her ached. In her room, she sat on the bed, eased off her shoes and lay back with her eyes closed. She couldn't hear Natalie anymore, but she was sure the woman would rave on and on, banking on Melissa's reluctance to betray her sister's part in the charade.

The worst of it was that Jeremy would listen.

CHAPTER NINE

MELISSA'S THOUGHTS WERE SO chaotic she didn't expect to drop off to sleep, but she must have. She was dragged back into consciousness by a tattoo of knocks she ignored.

"It's Brian. I'm coming in." He was a cutout of black construction paper in the half-light. The bed creaked as he sat down beside her. "How do you feel?"

"Fantastic," she muttered. "I never felt better."

He groped for her hand and pressed his lips to each of her fingertips in turn. But as he bent to kiss her she turned her face away.

Whistling through clenched teeth, he stood up. "I knew that bastard would hurt you. I'm going over and wipe up the floor with him."

"Forget it. It wouldn't help." Brian was built like a football player, but Jeremy wasn't exactly a ninety-pound weakling. It was anybody's guess who would wipe up the floor with whom. Either way, the trouble would be laid at her doorstep.

"It would help me," he insisted. "I feel partially responsible for your being here."

"Remind me to take a poke at you when I get my strength back."

He grinned and then looked very serious. "I think you should go back to Albany in the morning."

"No."

"Why not? I'll keep an eye on your sister for you. Then when this nightmare is over, we'll get together again, pretend none of this ever happened and start fresh. How about it? Can I help you pack?"

Albany. Home. Rush-hour traffic. Shopping. Even Mr. Lowell and his speeches. It sounded too good to be true. It was. "I can't leave before the recital on Friday. Arlene would never forgive me."

He rolled his eyes toward the ceiling. "When are you going to stop thinking about your sister and start thinking about—"

"Brian, please!" She'd heard the argument too many times before.

"Okay." He held up one hand, recognizing defeat. "I have another idea."

She grimaced. "No more ideas."

"We'll take that tour of the countryside in the morning. Stay out all day. We won't come back until Nat has already gone to whatever bash is on the agenda. You won't have to see hide nor hair of her."

"If I steal you away from the day's activities, it'll only give her another thing to rage at me about."

"We don't have to leave together. If you'd rather, we can meet somewhere." He dropped to his knees beside the bed. "How does it sound?"

"I don't know." With tomorrow filled to the brim, she'd have only the fashion show the next day and the recital at night and she'd be free to go home. But then, there was Brian to be considered. He'd already gotten the wrong idea about how she felt about him.

"If we keep it to just two good friends having a carefree day?" he asked, picking up on her train of thought.

Grateful to him, she nodded. "The idea of staying clear of your sister for a whole day is irresistible."

"Good. Let's say we meet on the beach below the Sea View restaurant at eight in the morning."

"Make that ten, and you're on."

"You look tense. I could give you a rubdown before I go." His eyes skimmed her slim length, and there was enough of a glint in them to remind Melissa that his feelings weren't brotherly.

"I think I need sleep more than I need a massage. But thanks anyway."

"I'm told I have the magic touch."

"No, thanks."

He slapped a hand against his thigh. "Guess I can't win 'em all."

"Good night, Brian," she said softly, reaching up to cover the yawn she couldn't stifle.

"I take it that's my exit cue?"

"No offense meant."

"None taken," he assured her, backing toward the door. "See you soon."

She slept badly, opening her eyes every hour or so to find that it was still dark, until at last, mercifully, the first lemony rays of morning sun told her she could get up. She'd look in on Eli and Murphy before she met with Brian, she decided. If everything went as planned, she probably wouldn't have another chance.

Hurriedly she washed, dressed and brushed her hair. It was stubborn and every which way, reflecting her erratic mood, but she managed to tame it enough to sleek it back with enameled clips. The cuckoo clock sounded, startling her as she crept down the stairs, but she didn't cry out. The floor didn't creak, and the door didn't slam. So far, so good.

When she reached the shack, Eli threw open the door and ushered her in, as if he had been expecting her and she'd arrived unconscionably late. There was no time for niceties and little for explanations. Someone had just brought him a torn and bleeding yellow warbler taken from a cat, and the newcomer required his full attention. Melissa would have to see to the needs of the other patients as best she could.

With rolled-up sleeves and the canvas coverall apron Eli provided, she set to work gratefully. It was good to feel useful and even better to be too busy to indulge in self-pity and wishful thinking.

By the time Eli had sponged the wounds, applied salve and settled Tracy the warbler into a nest of leaves in a cardboard carton, Melissa had finished with the cages and refilled all the seed and water containers. The two were able to sit down with feelings of satisfaction and accomplishment to scalding cups of herbal tea and squares of shortbread.

"He'll make it," Eli said, nodding. "He's a real little battler. That's what Tracy means, 'he who does battle with bravery.'"

Murphy had been given the run of the kitchen for the last two days, it seemed. He'd graduated to the screened flying cage and was ready to be set free.

The thought sobered her. Melissa could only think of the many perils that lay waiting in the outside world.

"Ah, yes. Wind, weather, other birds. Human beings—his worst enemies, I'm afraid. I know. He knows. But he's a free spirit. Imprisonment would be the cruelest punishment of all. If if hadn't been for Illona, he'd have made a devilish ruckus trying to escape before."

"Illona?" Melissa questioned. "You'll set them free at the same time?"

"I will. The lad's made his choice."

"And if Illona has other ideas?"

Eli, missing the teasing in his visitor's voice, drank deeply from his cup before answering. "It's harder to tell with that one. She's shy, but something of a coquette. I can only hope she feels the same. We'll know soon. Tomorrow, if it doesn't rain. The next day, if it's clear."

"I'll be leaving, myself," Melissa told him, recognizing the moment had come to let him know. "I really only came over to tell you and Murphy goodbye."

He looked genuinely distressed. "How does Jeremiah feel about this?"

"Jeremy?" His question took her by surprise. "He doesn't know yet."

"He won't like it."

She didn't know what to say. The two men were fast friends. She couldn't very well tell Eli that it was Jeremy who was driving her away. "If he notices I'm gone at all, his reaction will be one of relief."

"He'll notice. And he won't like it."

"We didn't exactly hit it off, he and I." To put it mildly.

"You hit it off all right. You hit him right between the eyes. I could tell from the first. Before I met you. Just hearing him tell about you bringing Murphy here. But Jeremy's peculiar. Keeps his feelings to himself. Because he's been alone for so many years, I'd wager."

"You've been alone," she said, seizing the opportunity to suggest that he put aside the past and make a future for himself in the world of the living. "It hasn't embittered you."

"I'm never alone." He made a sweeping gesture with one hand to call her attention to the never-ending twittering, chirping and squawking that filled the room.

"As much as you love your little people, Eli," she told him gently, "they aren't human beings."

"Thank the Lord for that!" he guffawed. "I have all the human beings I want. There's Jeremiah and one or two others who come by now and again. They jaw awhile and bring me something to read or something fresh baked. A man doesn't need more than a handful of good friends, does he? And now I have you."

"But I'm leaving."

"You'll be back."

"No." She caught her lower lip between her teeth. "That is, maybe just once more before I leave. If I can. To see Murphy and—"

"We'll see." His eyes twinkled. "Don't waste good sympathy on me, Melissa. I have memories. Memories enough to last several lifetimes. I'm a fortunate man."

The visit was over too soon. Brian would be wondering where she was, if he'd arrived on schedule. Reluctantly she made her way down to the beach. As she sat waiting, her knees drawn up to her chin, she pondered what Eli had said. He was a fortunate man. He had memories. Did Jeremy have memories? Were they good ones?

Lost in thought, she wasn't aware of Jeremy's approach until he stood over her, and she had to dig her hands into the sand to control their movement.

"I was on my way to Eli's when I saw you," he said. "You make quite a picture sitting here, looking out over the water, your hair blowing. You love the sea, don't you?"

She nodded. "When I was a little girl we used to vacation at the seashore. Never enough to suit me, though. My grandfather had been a sailor," she went on, her words tumbling out too fast, betraying her agitation at the unexpected meeting. "He told me that when the wind was high and the breakers were crashing, it was the water sprites doing battle. I ached with all my heart to lie all night, covered with sand, except for my head, and fall asleep, hearing the roar of the surf."

"And did you?" Jeremy knelt beside her.

"I couldn't get my father's permission."

"If you were the same as a little girl as you are as a big one, I'm surprised to hear you didn't do it anyway."

"I was docile as a child," she said, carefully measuring her reactions.

"What happened to change you?"

The edge of sarcasm gave her the strength she needed to lock eyes with him. "I grew up."

"So I see."

He looked tired and rather pale, but stirringly appealing all the same. An empty ache began in her middle as she realized that after today or possibly tomorrow she would never see him again. She would never hear his voice or experience his kiss.

With a small gasp, she forced such thoughts to the shadowy edges of her consciousness where they belonged. She should be celebrating. Soon she'd be free of the York hegemony. "You probably flatter yourself that I came looking for you."

"No," he said. "I didn't think that."

"You did once."

"As you say, I was flattering myself and indulging in some wishful thinking." He looked to one side and then the other. They were alone. There wasn't a sail on the horizon. "Are you waiting for someone?"

"Brian. He's late."

"He'll be here." Jeremy pressed his lips together. "I deliberately watched for you this morning, hoping you'd come. We should talk."

She ignored his suggestion and looked pointedly at the paper bag he carried. Unmistakably it held a wine bottle. Several magazines were tucked under his arm, as well.

"Gifts for Eli?"

He nodded.

"With a friend like you, he doesn't need enemies."

"Meaning?"

"A friend wouldn't encourage his drinking."

He stood up, his face changing ever so slightly as he teetered on the edge of an angry retort. Trying for good behavior wasn't easy for him. "You know Eli. Can't you weigh what you've seen against the loose talk? Does he seem like a staggering drunk to you?"

Now it was Melissa's turn to bristle. "Not all alcoholics are staggering drunks," she said.

"You're right, of course," he admitted. "But your accusation put me off. I wish I knew where those damn rumors about him got started. Eli isn't an alcoholic. This is a special blackberry wine I pick up for him sometimes. He enjoys a glass of it occasionally before he goes to bed. It helps his circulation." He walked a few paces, then came back and rammed his hands into the pockets of his windbreaker. His tirade was evidently not finished. "It makes me mad as hell. People talk about him because he doesn't wear a tie, complain about the weather or attend town meetings."

"Maybe you should encourage him to do that.

"Complain about the weather?"

"He should get out more. He's a dear, wonderful person. He has much to contribute, and he's wasting it."

"Wasting it? I could name more than a few important people who wouldn't agree with you. He's a respected authority on birds. He's had two books and countless articles published on the things he's learned about them. One is in here, if you care to read it."

As he knelt beside her and began flipping through the pages of one of the magazines, her senses responded predictably. Her inner woman, wild with longing, nagged at her to throw pride to the wind and accept as much or as little as he was willing to offer, and gratefully.

The scene that might follow her surrender whirled across her mind. She and Jeremy would make love there on the sand, oblivious to the maelstrom of waves breaking around them.

"Do you want to?" he asked.

She warmed as he looked at her quizzically. "Do I want to—what?"

"Read the article."

Very well. His presence disquieted her. All the logic in the world couldn't change that. It would take time and distance. "Not now," she answered, dismissing his attempt to show her the magazine. "I'll pick up a copy of my own later. I'd like to have it to keep."

"Eli isn't like everyone else. Being a nonconformist yourself to some extent, you should respect that. He's living the way he chooses to live. Isn't that what happiness is all about?"

"You've made your point."

"Is that what I'm trying to do, do you suppose? Make points?"

"I can't say what you're trying to do, but I'm tired of having you pounce on each word I say and tear it apart."

He closed the magazine, rolled it up and slapped it against his other hand in frustration. "You're right. I have no justifiable quarrel with you."

"I wish you'd go." She hugged her knees and sat with her forehead resting on them.

"Melissa, I don't want it to be this way."

"Please!"

"Afraid Hendricks will come and find me here?"

Until he'd said it, she hadn't given a thought to Brian's certain reaction to discovering her with Jeremy. The men might even come to blows. Now she was more anxious than ever that he go. "Just do me one last favor and leave."

"We might get some rain," he said, looking over the water. "If we do, you might see your water sprites in action."

"I won't be here long enough."

"It's easy to feel a kinship with the ocean," he went on as if he hadn't heard her. "They say the turbulence of the sky and water is much like the turbulence in men's souls."

It was an odd remark for him to have made under the circumstances. "That's true of men who are changeable and inconstant," she said archly.

He didn't answer but caught up a strand of her hair and rubbed it between his fingers, as a buyer of cloth might do to determine the thread content. "Few things are as beautiful as a woman's hair. I should have asked you to clip off a lock for me."

She jerked her head away and glared at him. "If you're planning to make a doll to stick pins into, won't you need nail parings as well?"

He didn't smile. He didn't even look self-satisfied or cocky. Such deep pain crept into his eyes that for an instant all bitterness between them was erased.

"I wish the circumstances of our meeting could have been different," he said in a voice that was no more than a whisper.

Translated, that meant he wished her father was an oil magnate, Melissa decided. Or that she had the knack of spinning straw into gold. She almost wished she had. Swallowing a painful lump in her throat, she dragged her eyes away from his. "People make their own circumstances."

"That's true, I suppose," he said, after a long pause. He turned then and walked away the way he had come.

He was hardly out of sight when Brian arrived, huffing and puffing and full of apologies for being late. As he helped her into the car, she worked hard at sounding enthusiastic about their day—even harder to keep from crying.

The road wound past green hills fragrant with pine. It plunged past glistening lakes, then dipped into fertile valleys and eased through sleepy, all-but-forgotten villages. Much of the way was bordered with bluebells and mountain laurel. The meadows were now golden with buttercup, then white with daisies. After snacking at an old inn that had once been a stagecoach stop, they investigated the thunderous roar of a waterfall and strolled along the water's edge picking wildflowers.

Without warning, Brian planted a kiss on top of her head. Why couldn't she feel for him something of what she felt for Jeremy?

"Melissa. Sweet Melissa." His voice was thick with emotion as he repeated her name, as if to reassure himself that he was really holding her.

Alerted to danger, she tensed. It was wrong—terribly wrong—to pretend to feel more for Brian than she did. She would only be using him, as she had been used.

"A friend of mine has a cabin near here," he said. "We could—"

"No. We couldn't," she broke in, her voice soft, but allowing no argument.

"I was afraid of that."

"Brian..." The atmosphere seemed charged, each of their breaths measured. How could she make him understand without hurting him?

"Uh—how about a swim?" he tried. "Somewhere."

"A swim would be fine. Anywhere."

"How about Tahiti?" He'd managed it. He'd bounced back and was himself again.

Their brief swim was followed by a shopping spree, in which they went their separate ways and returned with outlandish purchases. Brian bought Melissa a black stuffed kitten he claimed looked exactly like her because of its huge green eyes. She bought him a beanie with a pinwheel that whirled madly as he walked.

After a delectable seafood dinner at a restaurant that had once been a boat, they sat on the bank and watched the sun set.

From somewhere far off came a faint trill. As it grew louder, Melissa spotted the grayish flash of a bird she couldn't identify. Its song swelled as it soared above the treetops, then grew fainter again until it died away entirely, leaving her with a feeling of sweet sadness.

It seemed to have touched Brian, too. His eyes were fixed as if on something seen only by him. It was then the thought struck her. She'd been incredibly self-centered. Despite all their hours together, she knew next to nothing about him. She'd make up for it now by questioning him about his work, his ambitions and his dreams. To her surprise, his answers were evasive.

She jokingly accused him of being first, a private eye; second, a secret agent; and last, a Mafia hit man. He laughed and told her she was right on all three counts. "I like to keep busy," he teased.

He was also a practiced changer-of-subjects, she concluded. By the time they'd said good-night and she had shut herself in her room, she realized that she knew little more about him than she'd known the day they met.

CHAPTER TEN

HAD ANYONE PREDICTED at eight o'clock the next morning that by one in the afternoon she'd be nibbling finger sandwiches and sipping tea, watching a parade of fashions she would never be able to afford, Melissa would have denied it vehemently. Yet here she was.

Her plan had been a seemingly simple one. She would hibernate in her room until everyone had gone wherever they were going. Still in her robe, she'd enjoy a late but leisurely breakfast, pack her suitcase and be sinfully idle until it was time to get ready for her last Sandgate appearance—the talent show that night.

She might have guessed her sister would have other ideas.

"It isn't just a skip and a twirl down a runway, Missy," the girl argued. "The fashion show's going to be spectacular. There's live music. The spotlight effects are unbelievable, and there'll be photographers from every newspaper within a hundred miles."

The segment Arlene would grace was called "Night and Day," and, as could be expected, all the costumes would be white or black. The girl would be wearing a white evening suit with beaded satin lapels.

"The skirt is so slim, I practically have to lie on the floor to wriggle into it."

"It sounds frightfully uncomfortable."

"Who expects to be beautiful and comfortable at the same time?" she reasoned philosophically. "Wait till you see Mama dear. She's all ruffles in black tulle."

"Natalie?"

"Yes. It's a mother-daughter thing, you know. But she'll be in too much of a nervous tizzy to even see you. I promise. You can wear dark glasses, slide in and take a back table."

"I forgot to bring my trench coat. Besides, I'm leaving in the morning," Melissa said as she sensed herself weakening. "I don't want to see anyone."

"You don't have to worry about Jeremy."

The girl's comment jarred her. Did she guess what had gone on between Jeremy and her? "You can guarantee that?"

"Absolutely. You know perfectly well men detest this kind of thing. Todd has headed for the hills, and even Brian is begging off."

"I don't know." Melissa had seen her sister model more than a few times at the department store. But this did sound like something she'd hate to miss.

"I'll do the dishes for a month," Arlene threw in, deciding to cinch the argument. "Oh, Missy, I want you there."

So here she was, and everything was fairly much as her sister had promised. With one small difference. Jeremy wasn't as phobic about women's style shows as Melissa's sister had expected he would be. He sat only four tables away, looking dashing enough in his dark gray sports jacket to knock her off her feet all over again. In spite of Melissa's efforts to hide behind the floral centerpiece, he'd noticed her minutes after his arrival with his breathlessly excited mother-in-law on his arm.

Melissa might have been sitting too close to an open fire, judging by the uncomfortable hotness that spread over her, tempting her to sprint for the door, explanations be damned. But by turning her chair at a slight angle to the table, she was able to pretend not to notice when Jeremy favored her with a nod of recognition. With all the courage she could muster, she stared at the platform, grateful, at least, for the dim lighting.

The opening segment was called only "Seasons," and each quarter year was represented with appropriate costumes and spotlights. There were swimsuits and hostess dresses, tennis outfits and ball gowns. The emcee was entertaining, and the scenery would have done credit to a professional stage production.

Natalie opened the "Night and Day" segment in a dress that was soft and flowing, yet elegant and sensual. Arlene, whose dark curls had been sleeked and fastened with a looped hairpiece, earned a ripple of oohs and aahs from the audience and dozens of pencils set to work as women made notes of the white evening suit for possible purchase.

"This seat isn't taken, is it?" Jeremy asked.

Out of the corner of her eye, Melissa had seen him rise and move toward her, closer—closer. Still she clutched the table with a start when she heard his voice, losing the presence of mind to tell him she expected a luncheon companion at any moment. Then it was too late. He was seated beside her.

"I'd rather hoped to run into you last night," he said.

According to the schedule Natalie had tacked in the hallway, there had been a gala dinner-dance at the country club. "I had other plans," she said.

"I can't say that I blame you. The evening was topped off with a yesterday-and-today slide show.

Sandgate and its inhabitants then and now. Hard enough for the locals to sit still for."

"I can imagine."

"I thought at first you might have stayed away to avoid me," he said, tapping a finger lightly against the stem of his water glass. "But I'd be flattering myself again, wouldn't I?"

His finger tapping grew more rhythmic as silence fell between them. Someone was singing "Unforgettable" in a deep Bing Crosby baritone. A red-haired girl floated down the runway wearing a shimmering blue-green evening dress. She stopped, smiled and turned to look at Jeremy over her shoulder before moving on.

"Hey, you two." Melissa's sister, her eyelashes beaded looking, dropped into the chair across from Jeremy. "My part is over, thank goodness. I'm famished. Missy, are you going to finish that chicken salad sandwich?"

"Help yourself," Melissa said.

"Thanks. Jeremy, you are the very last person I expected to see here."

"I'm the last person I expected to see here, too," he admitted. "But the forecast said rain, and Winifred is afraid to drive when the streets are wet."

"And you got lassoed into the job of chauffeuring before you had a chance to escape." She helped herself to the pickle slices on Melissa's plate.

Jeremy gave her a slow smile. "Something like that."

"The forecast was right. It's raining cats." Clapping a hand onto Melissa's wrist, she nodded toward the retreating model in blue-green. "That's the dress I wanted you to see. Isn't it a knockout?"

"It's very nice," Melissa agreed, not really seeing anything. She was aware only of Jeremy sitting beside her.

"*Nice,* did you say?" Her sister laughed. "The table setting is nice. The chicken salad is nice. The dress is— is breathtaking."

"All right. It's beautiful."

"And it would be perfect for you. It *is* you."

"It'll have to learn to be someone else." Melissa had to smile. Did her sister have any idea how much the dress cost? "Unfortunately I just spent my last million."

"Let me buy it for you," Jeremy offered.

"Don't be ridiculous," Melissa snapped, too surprised by his unexpected and insulting gesture to refuse more politely. The way his thought processes worked, he'd suppose they had set up the scene together, hoping to wangle a dress out of him.

"Jean is right. It would be lovely on you."

"I've already given you my answer."

"This isn't your ordinary situation. The proceeds go to charity."

"And I'm one of you favorite charities?"

"Now *you're* flattering yourself, sweetheart," he threw at her. "Don't be so self-righteous. You're misreading my motives."

"I don't think so."

"Everything does go to charity, Missy," her sister said. "One hundred percent."

"Then let him buy the dress for his mother-in-law."

Jeremy's mouth tightened. "Winifred has already bought two dresses."

"A woman can't have too many dresses, can she?" Melissa asked with saccharine sweetness.

"My point exactly. Won't you change your mind? I'd like to buy something."

"Then buy the black for Natalie."

He tightened his hand into a fist and dropped it onto the table. It struck a spoon, and the spoon clattered to the floor. Several heads turned toward them. "Why the hell should I buy a dress for Natalie?"

"I don't know. Should you?"

Her sister's surprise at the bitter exchange between them was evident. "It's sweet of you to make the offer, Jeremy," she said in her exaggerated, smoothing-things-over voice. "But Missy is terribly independent."

"I'm not trying to compromise her," he growled. "The other night her dress was ruined because of my gardener's carelessness. It's only right that I replace it."

"He has a point," the girl said.

Jeremy lowered his chin, reminding Melissa of a raging bull about to charge. "When you didn't turn up at the dance last night, I thought perhaps it was because—"

"Because I'd torn my only dress?"

"I'm sure you have other dresses. But women don't always pack several gowns when they go on a short trip."

"That's true," her sister sang.

"I come prepared," Melissa assured him.

"Prepared for taking a tumble into a muddy ditch?"

"Prepared for any eventuality."

"Shall we talk about the weather?" Arlene asked.

Jeremy pushed his chair back. "I'll have the dress sent over to you," he said.

"I won't wear it."

"I don't give a damn if you dress a bloody scarecrow in it and stick it in your backyard." He stood up. "I enjoyed watching you in the fashion show, Jean," he said, composing himself with effort.

"Why are you trying to sabotage everything?" her sister cried when he had stalked away.

Melissa held up one hand. "Don't you start on me."

"Why not? I go out of my way to win Jeremy over for Todd's sake and you have to start World War Three with him."

"It was your deserting us in Mystic that set him off. He began yelling gold-digger, and I lost my temper. Baby, he's never going to put his stamp of approval on you."

"Not the way you're antagonizing him."

"The fact that I exist antagonizes him." Melissa leaned forward and took her sister's hand. "Let's both go home. We don't need Natalie's money. We'll find another way to pay for your part of the trip to Greece, if I have to take a Saturday job."

Defiance showed in her sister's eyes. "I'm not going to budge. I'm having a wonderful time. I love Todd, and he loves me. Nothing anybody says is going to change that."

"So you're going to live happily ever after?"

"As a matter of fact, we are."

Melissa sighed. Now it was anybody's guess what would happen. Jeremy had said it. What has common sense got to do with being in love?

"It can't work, baby. Jeremy will cut Todd out of the family business if you're in the picture. He told me as much."

"I couldn't care less about the company or the York money. If Todd's thrown out, he'll make good somewhere else. Besides, I didn't say we were going to run off and get married." Arlene looked toward the platform. Off to the side, a blond girl in a cinnamon-colored pantsuit beckoned to her. "We're going to see each other, though," she said, rising slowly, "wherever and whenever we please. Nobody's going to stop us. Not even you."

CHAPTER ELEVEN

THE "NO-TALENT" SHOW, as Brian dubbed it, followed his predictions closely, with everyone squeezed into costumes they'd worn twenty years and forty pounds ago. There were jugglers, mimes and tap dancers, along with a one-man band and a magician whose colored handkerchiefs refused to unknot themselves on cue. A woman in a chicken suit clucked through an interminable rendition of "Be My Love," and a dignified-looking man in a pinstriped suit did impersonations of Edward G. Robinson and Elvis Presley.

Arlene's Chopin recital stole the show, however, and after a stunned silence, the applause was deafening. Tears of pride stung Melissa's eyes as she listened to the encores the audience demanded. Maybe everything—all of it—was worth it. Just for that moment.

Even Brian, who sat beside her through the show, seemed awed by the girl's ability. "Quite a sister you have there, kitten," he whispered when it was over and people were filing out. "Where did she learn to attack the ivories like that?"

"Darned if I know. We had the same piano teacher."

"Maybe your talents lie elsewhere."

"I'll let you know if I find them."

"Maybe I'd prefer to discover them for myself."

Even as she took in Brian's gentle teasing, Melissa found herself searching the auditorium, row by row, for

Jeremy. At first she supposed he hadn't come. It would be difficult to imagine him suffering through an aria from the third act of *Carmen* or a stilted reading of *The Rime of the Ancient Mariner*.

Then she saw him, and the tears that had only threatened before now filled her eyes. He was alone in the last row, still seated after almost everyone had begun to leave. Why was it that when they were apart for a few hours she could remember only the good things?

Goodbye, Jeremy, she whispered inside herself.

"Ready to go?" Brian asked.

"As soon as I go backstage and congratulate Arlene."

"Right." He ran interference for her as they worked their way down the center aisle and cut to the right to reach the stage. "Everyone has the same idea, I think. You have a celebrity on your hands."

Past the burly man who was acting as stage manager and the animal trainer who was attempting to lure his star poodle into its carrying cage, Melissa's sister and Natalie stood together, obviously in heated debate. They spoke quietly, but it wasn't necessary to hear the words to know they were quarreling bitterly.

"Hold it, kitten." Brian wheeled about to take both Melissa's arms and steer her back the way they had come. "I think the situation calls for retreat."

"But—"

"The girl's holding her own from what I can tell. And somehow I don't think she'd appreciate the interruption."

"Maybe you're right," Melissa agreed, remembering the things her sister had said to her earlier.

"Thatta girl. Wait here. I'll get you some punch."

"Melissa, isn't it?" Winifred Havelock's icy fingers closed on Melissa's upper arm, sending shivers through her.

"Yes."

"Natalie's daughter is a miracle, isn't she? An absolute miracle. How can anyone so lovely to look at be so talented as well? I'm having a few friends in later. Do you think she'll agree to play for us?"

"I'm sure she will." Melissa knew that as keyed up as her sister was after a performance, it would be hard to keep her from playing.

"You'll come, too, won't you?" Jeremy's mother-in-law wasn't a beautiful woman. Her skin was as pale as parchment, and her eyes were too large for her fragile face. They were round and moist as if she were always on the brink of tears. Still, she was attractive.

"I hadn't planned on—"

"We haven't had a chance to get acquainted. I've heard that you paint."

"A little. Just for my own amusement."

"My daughter painted, too. She said it was therapeutic."

"Yes, it is."

"She painted mostly landscapes and flowers. There were too many ugly paintings in the world, she said. I'd like to show you some of her work. Please come," she added before joining her friends.

"Not a bad old girl, that one," Brian said, handing Melissa the glass of punch he'd gotten for her. "For her kind, that is."

"She's invited me to a party," Melissa told him.

"You aren't going, are you?" he asked sharply.

"I might put in an appearance. I don't want to hurt her feelings."

"I don't think it's a good idea. You wanted to get an early start in the morning, remember?"

"I have to see Ar—I mean, Jean before I go. I'll probably be able to catch her there. I won't stay long."

"Hmm." He looked at her sideways, took a sip of punch and grimaced. "What's in this? Or maybe I should ask what isn't in it. Darned if it isn't just fruit punch."

"What did you expect?" Melissa giggled. "You look as if you've been poisoned."

"I think I have been. The organizers should realize that we deserve something with a kick to it after what they've put us through."

WINIFRED HAVELOCK had said she was having "a few people" in. Her buffet table was piled high enough to accommodate the entire audience from the auditorium and then some. Puzzled at not seeing Jeremy and perturbed that her sister hadn't arrived yet, Melissa picked at a salad she'd built and sat down to listen as an elderly man and his wife sang a medley of Victor Herbert love songs.

Still no Jeremy. Still no Arlene. And no Todd. It was impossible to ignore the connection. Something warned her that she should go back to the house.

After making her presence known to her hostess, who was too busy with her other guests to insist that she stay, Melissa located Brian, who'd armed himself with a glass of something potent looking to take away the taste of the fruit punch.

"I'll take you home," he said. "Wait until I locate Nat. Have you seen her?"

"Not in the past half hour. But there are so many people coming and going it's hard to pin anyone down.'' Melissa reached for his hand and pressed it. "I wouldn't want you to bother, anyway. I've brought my own car. It's back to the house and straight to bed for me. I'm leaving for Albany at the crack of dawn.''

"You're sure?''

"I'm sure.''

He touched his fingers to his lips, then touched them to hers. "Till I see you in Albany, then.''

She made the drive along the sea road, without looking toward the water. All her life the sights, the smells and the sounds of the seashore had brought her an inexplicable inner joy. Now all those things, still filled with the same beauty, would only evoke a kind of sadness.

The phone was ringing as she let herself into the house.

"Oh, Missy, thank goodness it's you.'' Her sister's voice sounded breathy and faraway. "I was going to hang up if *Mother darling* answered.''

"Where are you?''

"I'm with Todd.''

"I might have guessed. But where?''

There was a long silence, and Melissa could hear her sister whispering to someone in the background. "Don't be mad, Missy,'' Arlene said at last. "Todd and I are getting married.''

"Married!'' Melissa pressed the receiver closer to her ear, hoping desperately that she'd heard wrong. "When?''

"Now. Immediately. Natalie and I had a gigantic row. Maybe you heard. She said some horrible things to me. I couldn't have stayed in that house if she'd paid me ten times the amount. Todd was so sweet and comforting, I—''

"I don't care how sweet he was. Married? Just like that?"

"It's called eloping, Missy," the girl said, getting defensive. "And it's terribly romantic. It isn't a crime."

"It will be, where Mother and Dad are concerned."

"We love each other terribly. What's the point in waiting? I know I promised you I wouldn't do anything sudden. But this isn't sudden. Not really. It's as if Todd and I have known each other for years. He's known all about me right from the start. So there are no secrets between us. I won't have to give up my music, either. Todd is proud of me. He's behind me all the way."

The girl chattered on and on about Todd and about how happy they were going to be. How happy she was already. Melissa didn't interrupt. She didn't dare. She might say something she'd regret later.

"Are you sure about this?" she asked when Arlene had run out of words.

"I'm sure." The girl's voice was quivery now. It wouldn't take much to have her in tears. Right or wrong, Melissa didn't want to be responsible for that. Not on her sister's wedding day. "Please say you're happy for me."

"I am happy, honey. It's just—so unexpected. I feel cheated. I would have wanted to be there."

"You will be. I promise. We'll have a proper ceremony later. You can get all prettied up and give me away or do whatever sisters do at weddings."

"They cry," Melissa said, blinking back tears that had begun already.

"I advise you to leave Sandgate as soon as you can," Arlene said. "Natalie is going to be livid."

"Does she know about your plans?"

"She knows I'm with Todd, and she'll probably put two and two together after the things I told her at the auditorium."

"I'm driving home in the morning but—"

"I have to run now," Arlene broke in. "Please forgive me for the frightful things I said to you earlier. I didn't really mean them. I'll be in touch soon. And drive home carefully. It's raining, you know."

So Natalie was going to be livid. Great. Melissa considered a hasty change of plans. She could drive home tonight, or she could seek out a motel—out of the line of Natalie's fire.

But no. There wouldn't be a vacancy anywhere in Sandgate this week, and it was too late and too wet to be driving any long distances. At least, she could be in bed when the woman came home.

She shampooed her hair as quickly as she could and was towel drying it when a quick knock at the door announced a visitor. Who? Natalie certainly wouldn't knock. Brian wouldn't, either. Her pulses quickened when she lifted a corner of the curtain and saw Jeremy's car.

"Just a minute," she called, slipping a robe over her shorty nightgown and tying its sash securely.

The knock came again. More urgent this time. But she willed herself not to hurry. She smoothed her hair back from her forehead, pinned it into place and opened the door.

He strode past her, his hair wet and shaggy from the rain, and clicked on the kitchen light. After checking the bathroom, he turned to her and jammed his hands into the pockets of his windbreaker. It didn't take much imagination to decide that he wasn't in one of his more tender moods.

"Where's Hendricks?"

She struggled to keep her temper in check. "Why don't you run along upstairs and look under the beds?"

"Are you alone?"

"What do you think?"

He crossed to the window and yanked the curtain aside. "Wretched weather. Has anyone been here?"

"Anyone?"

"Todd. Have you seen him?"

So that was it. He suspected that Melissa was somehow involved with hiding the two lovers. She wished now she hadn't opened the door to him. "You really ought to think about hiring a private detective to keep track of your brother if his whereabouts are so important to you."

"Do you have any coffee?" His shoulders slumped, and he looked weary.

"I can make some. Instant."

"Thanks." He sat on the edge of the couch and raked his fingers through his hair. "What about Jean?"

"What about her?" She didn't plan to help him. He'd have to come out and tell her what was on his mind. Maybe if he formed his fears into words, he'd see how ridiculous they were.

As he sprang up again and came toward her, wildeyed, she began to wish she hadn't baited him. Then she saw that it wasn't rage in his eyes. It was deep concern. "I'm not here to quarrel with you, Melissa. I—I don't know why it always comes to that when we're together. It shouldn't. I've wanted everything to be right with you, of all people. But at this moment, I can only think about Todd. I have to find him before..."

He didn't finish what he'd started to say, but she could have finished it for him. To Jeremy, a serious relationship between the two was unthinkable. Melissa couldn't hate him for that. He was a born snob. He couldn't help himself any more than he could help the color of his eyes or the set of his jaw.

"She called a little while ago," she volunteered.

"Jean? Where is she?"

"I don't know," she answered truthfully.

"Is she with Todd?"

"She was. I don't know if she is now," she hedged. "Maybe if you'd go home, you might hear from him."

He sat down again heavily and picked up one of the knickknacks on the table, fingering it absently. "If you knew anything of their plans, would you tell me?"

"No," she answered truthfully. "Do you want me to take your jacket? It's soaked."

He waved her away and set down the figurine he'd been holding. "I'll be going in a minute."

"Let me fix that coffee for you first."

"Don't bother."

"No bother. I could use a cup myself."

"All right then."

He was being as foolish and unreasonable as a small boy who was used to getting his own way. But for no good reason, the sight of him suffering tugged at her heart. She would have liked to have been able to put her arms around him and offer comfort.

He'd been brought up with an unshakable sense of separateness of social classes. A York was several cuts above the average man. He would have been better off living in a different century. No wonder he envied Eli the simple life. A York couldn't give in to the yearnings of his heart. If those yearnings were for someone who wasn't listed in the social register.

"My—friend didn't attend a fancy finishing school, it's true," she said carefully, trying to pave the way for her sister. "But she doesn't slurp her soup and she doesn't eat peas with a knife. She knows how to dress, and she uses reasonably good grammar. She would never be an embarrassment to you or to your family. If you could only see beyond your prejudices, you'd know that she has more than a few wonderful qualities. And I can assure you that her interest in Todd is not based on the size of his bank account. He could do a lot worse, and he'd have a hard time doing better."

There! She'd said it. The rest—heaven help them— the revelation about the masquerade and the girl's true identity, would come later. And Melissa hoped to be a good safe distance away.

"What are you talking about?" Jeremy snapped.

She dug her bare toes into the rug. So much for sympathy. She might have saved her breath. "I couldn't expect you to understand. But I hope Todd is different. I hope he's worth the love she feels for him."

"Sit down."

"I have to set the water on for coffee."

He made an impatient karatelike chop with one hand that might have severed the coffee table if it had struck an inch lower. "Forget the damn coffee. We have to talk."

Melissa held her ground. "We've had more than enough talking for one night."

"Please." He rested a hand on her arm and kept it there until she relented and sat beside him.

His eyes searched hers as though he hoped to read something in them. "Natalie hasn't told you the whole story. She couldn't, of course. Since you're close to Jean, you might somehow have let it slip."

"What story?" Melissa didn't melt with the new tenderness that flowed into his voice. It was designed to set her off balance, likely as not. She didn't understand his game, but experience had taught her some of his plays.

"Do you suppose I give a damn if Jean doesn't own the clothes on her back? Don't you think I'm fond of her, too? That doesn't count here. She and Todd must not—cannot—get involved. They can't fall in love, and they certainly can't marry."

It was ironic, she mused, that she should be the one to try to convince him to allow his brother to lead his own life. For as long as she could remember, people had been telling her the same thing about her sister. At least she and Jeremy had that much in common.

"Have you considered that you may have nothing to say in the matter? Your brother is an adult. You can't be there to protect him all his life."

"Protect him from Jean? For God's sake, Melissa." His face was ashen. His words came haltingly and without expression. "Jean is my daughter!"

CHAPTER TWELVE

MELISSA STARED AT HIM, too stunned to protest, as he stood, peeled off his jacket and flung it over the back of a chair. Clapping a hand to the back of his neck he rolled his head from one side to the other.

"Whiplash," he muttered, as if trying to decide how to say what had to be said. "Years ago. One of the roller coaster cars I was checking jolted against another and, well, it gives me hell whenever..."

His voice trailed off. The sound of the mantel clock ticking filled the room. Melissa sat quietly, not wanting to distract him from his fantastic story. Whatever it was, she had to know. It had begun as Natalie's deception. Now it was hers, as well.

He picked up her glass paperweight and transferred it absently from one hand to the other, setting the snowstorm into motion. "We were very young, Natalie and I, and in love with the idea of being in love. She was exquisitely beautiful, and my parents disapproved of her, which made her all the more exciting to me. We were inseparable. Then, all at once, she was gone. She didn't explain. She didn't come to see me. I couldn't even get her on the telephone. When she and her family moved away not long after that, I was devastated."

He spoke of his fury when his father finally admitted that he'd given Natalie a great deal of money to get out of Jeremy's life. Jeremy's first impulse had been to go after her. But when he'd thought it over, he'd realized how shallow her feelings for him must have been.

He picked up the paperweight again and shook it. He didn't speak until all the snow had settled. Sitting in silence, Melissa heard the rain outside. Drops fell steadily, rhythmically, and the branch of a pear tree outside the window made a scritching sound against the pane.

"Kathryn and I had known each other all our lives. She was a gentle sweet person who really knew how to listen, and she was there when I needed someone. When we announced our intention to marry, my parents were overjoyed. It was the match they'd hoped for."

He didn't learn until after his father's death that there had been more to the story. A child had been born to Natalie—a daughter, Jean. His daughter. When he'd gone over his father's accounts, trying to put things in order, it hadn't taken him long to wring the story out of the lawyer who'd been taking care of support payments.

"It was a nightmare," he said. "I loved my father and I missed him. But I hated him, too, for cheating me out of my daughter."

Immediately he got in touch with Natalie and proposed revealing the truth to Jean. She rejected the idea, pointing out that the girl could hardly be helped by discovering after so long that Natalie's husband, the man who had acted as the girl's father, was a pretender.

There was good reason for Natalie's nostalgic return to Sandgate, Jeremy explained. A music teacher in Europe. An incredibly expensive music teacher. Natalie had informed him that it was the burning desire of Jean's life to study with that music teacher. The lessons would take several years, and Jean couldn't possibly travel alone. Natalie had wanted to accompany her. The expenses of such a lengthy stay would be enormous. And Jeremy, not trusting Natalie's word, had wanted to see Jean's talent for himself before signing any cheques. With so many people attending the bicentennial, they'd decided it was the perfect opportunity for him to get to know Jean without arousing suspicion.

"The night we met," Melissa said, remembering the sudden change in Jeremy that had puzzled her, "and I said I was here with Natalie, you supposed I was Jean?"

A weary smile played on his lips. "The name was wrong. But then, I thought perhaps you'd learned the truth and were toying with me, pretending to be someone else. It was quite a shock. Up to that point, I'd been thinking some pretty unfatherly thoughts about you."

It was just her ill-fortune, Melissa thought miserably. Now that she felt closer than ever to him, when his moods had become understandable to her, and when she was finally able to admit to herself that she loved him, she had to reveal something to him that might alienate him forever.

"Natalie has been lying to you," she began, with a deep sigh. "We've all lied."

A chill moved through her when he raised his eyes to hers. "In what way have you lied? When you said you didn't know where Todd and Jean have gone? You must realize now how important . . ."

"Please don't say anything more until I've finished. This is going to be difficult enough."

So that she wouldn't have to face him and watch his despair turn to disgust, she rose and crossed to the window. A deafening crash of thunder followed a spear of lightning.

In spite of her discomfort, she almost laughed at the melodramatic effect. "Jean isn't your daughter."

He started to say something, but she waved her hands to silence him. "She isn't even Jean. Her name is Arlene Brandon, and she's my sister."

Now it was her turn to grope painfully for words that might explain without convicting. She kept her eyes riveted on a patch of light outside, where a muddy stream ran in an ever-widening path to the street below. The story unfolded itself in a disconnected way. It jolted ahead, then returned to fill in gaps and moved ahead again.

When it was over, she turned toward him and waited, knotting her fingers together and allowing her gaze to fall to the pattern of the braided rug. She had said everything she could think of to say. Why didn't he say something now?

A part of her considered making a dash for the door, climbing into her car and escaping. Maybe she would be able to blot out the last week from her memory, as she'd forgotten other painful scenes from childhood. Her best friend through kindergarten and elementary school had moved to Texas when she was ten. As Melissa had seen it then, the girl had abandoned her. She'd supposed she would never recover from the loss. She had. And so she would recover from Jeremy.

"Now you've decided to double-cross Natalie. Or would this be considered a triple cross?" His voice was razor sharp when he finally spoke. She wouldn't have recognized it. "Were you hired to captivate and distract me, so I wouldn't look into the scheme too closely?"

"I wasn't hired at all."

"Maybe you figure to profit more if your sister marries Todd. So you scrapped the original plan. Cute."

"It wasn't like that."

She took a step toward him, but he thrust out an arm to stop her. "Don't press your luck, sweetheart. If you come any closer, even that angel face won't keep me from throttling you."

"Won't you listen?"

"I hope for your sake you were well paid for your trouble. There'll be no marriage, I promise you." A blast of cold wind struck her in the face as he threw open the door and stared into the night. But if he'd planned to leave, he changed his mind. He turned back to her and kicked the door closed behind him. "Get dressed," he said, jerking his head toward the stairway. "And hurry up about it. Pack whatever you'll need for the night. I'm taking you home with me."

"But why?" She shivered and drew her robe more closely around her, as if the flimsy material could somehow protect her from his fury.

"Winifred loves guests, and that's what you'll be until I locate my brother. Consider it house arrest. Try to leave, and you'll be using your charms on the chief of police."

"How will you explain to your mother-in-law why I've come back?"

"You explain it." His laugh was a snarl. "Tell her you're afraid to stay alone in the storm. Tell her anything you like."

"She won't believe me."

"She'll believe you. She's too fine a woman to imagine you'd lie to her. Get moving now, or I'll drag you out the way you are." He took a threatening step toward her to reinforce his words. "And that would be even harder for you to explain."

WINIFRED WAS SO PLEASED at having unexpected company, she all but squealed. Without asking any questions, she had one of the servants ready a room. She didn't even puzzle over the vague excuse Jeremy gave for dashing out again as soon as he had delivered Melissa.

"If only I had known you were coming," the woman said, touching a finger to her chin. "We'd have had such a good time. But I've already taken a sleeping powder. Our visit will have to wait until morning."

Was it the luxuriantly piled white carpeting and the tightly closed shutters, Melissa wondered, or the sturdy way these houses had been built against the forces of nature that gave her room such an unnatural hush? Beyond the rose-tinted walls, she knew there were servants gliding down the corridors, tending to last-minute duties, yet it seemed that she was entirely alone and that the room was actually a beautifully furnished jail cell.

Would Jeremy be able to find Arlene and Todd? What would he do if he did? Then a thought came to her like an icicle pressed between her shoulder blades. What would he do if he didn't?

Even making an attempt at sleep seemed pointless. She tried to read a fashion magazine she'd found on the night table, but the pictures blurred before her eyes. Only static came over the radio. There was a supply of notepaper in the desk drawer, along with a ballpoint pen. Should she write an explanation for Jeremy? Would he read her words if he wouldn't listen to them?

She unfastened the hooks on the shutters, opened them and drew back the curtain, hoping the night would rush in and free her somehow. It was still raining. Not a violent rain now, but a hypnotic one. Time passed with agonizing slowness.

She saw the headlights long before the car approached and stopped. The driver got out, and he was alone. Her heart turned over and began thudding an uneven beat. She was listening now, though there was nothing to hear. Listening and waiting. When her bedroom door opened and closed soundlessly, she was still at the window.

"Natalie's cleared out," Jeremy said. "Hendricks too. But you knew that, didn't you?" He wiped the back of his hand across his mouth in a gesture of frustration. She couldn't make out his features in the dim light, but she could see the savage luminosity in his eyes, and she could hear his labored breathing. "You did your job well, little one."

"I had no job," she said numbly. "I only—"

"Went along for the ride?"

"You're soaking wet. Hadn't you better change? You'll catch a cold."

"Your concern is touching. But I can think of a more pleasant way to warm myself. I should get something for my time and money, wouldn't you say?"

She hardly heard him. Picking up an afghan that lay across the back of an overstuffed chair, she held it out to him. "At least put this around your shoulders." She was so nervous her voice quavered. But she recognized one slim hope. He was here. That was something. It might even mean he was ready to listen.

He let his arms drop to his sides in the stance of a gunfighter, waiting for his enemy to draw first. "Come here."

She stumbled toward him, as if the monotone in his voice had placed her in a trance. Snatching the afghan away, he hurled it across the room. It collided with the transistor radio and swept it to the floor.

"Kiss me the way you kissed me when we were in the woods."

When she didn't comply with his order at once, he yanked her against him. Her robe fell open with the impact and slid off one shoulder. She tried to adjust it, but he pulled her hand away.

"Have you really gone as far in entertaining me as you were instructed to go?" he asked. Gathering a fistful of hair, he eased her head back to make sure she took the full force of his shattering kiss. A kiss that was at once pain and pleasure, heaven and hell.

"What do you say to another picnic?" he muttered against her mouth.

A sob caught in her throat as he brought her head back again, to study her face. "You have every right to be bitter," she cried.

"It's good to know I have some rights. This time it'll be you and me as we really are. No game playing. No pretense. Can you manage that, Melissa? Your name really is Melissa, isn't it?"

She nodded mutely.

"A beacon of truth shines through the storm of deception." He relaxed his hold, allowing her to take her own weight, and she swayed, off balance.

"Not like this, Jeremy," she whispered, pleading with her eyes.

"Any way I want it to be. It's my picnic this time. I make the rules."

They stood face to face, gladiators, readying themselves for combat. The first move was his. His fingers splayed her narrow waist, then moved along the sides of her rib cage to find her breasts. When she gasped he raked her toward him again, bringing his scorching breath and insatiable mouth to the sensitive skin at the side of her neck.

If this was her penance, she thought, reeling drunkenly in the exquisite sensation that was hers, she almost welcomed it. She could only hope that when he'd played his role through, the bitterness would be gone. He would begin to feel what she was feeling now, an overpowering longing.

"Jeremy," she said softly, only wanting to hear the sound of his name in her ears.

"Damn you, I didn't have a chance," he snarled, sweeping her off her feet. When she uttered a faint protest, he only held her tighter. "Don't ever say no to me, little one," he warned, tearing back the quilt to deposit her sprawling on the bed. For what seemed to be an eternity, he stood staring down at her. "There's no hurry," he said thinly. "We have all the time we want, and I don't intend to overlook a square inch of you."

"The servants might have seen you come in," she tried.

He shook his head. "They're all asleep. And I was very discreet. Anything goes, doesn't it, as long as we're discreet?"

"Your mother-in-law."

"On nights like this, Winifred usually takes a sedative. I could set off a cannon and she wouldn't hear it." Impatient with the conversation, he slid smoothly over the foot of the bed to take his place beside her. Unmindful of the buttons, he discarded his shirt and shifted himself over her, the moist heat of his skin searing her breasts through the thin fabric of her night-gown.

True to his promise, he began his methodical and complete conquest, nipping at her earlobes lightly, tasting her forehead and brushing his mouth against her eyelids before laying claim to her pulsating lips again. All the while his hands made an exploration of their own, and his body pressed hers more deeply into the mattress.

"I love you," Melissa said. Though she'd meant to keep the words to herself, she was not sorry that they had burst forth.

All his movement stopped. It was as though a master switch that controlled him had been turned off. He exhaled sharply and looked down at her with the eyes of one who wanted with all his heart to believe.

"Oh, Melissa," he muttered, almost inaudibly. "Melissa." As if he needed to hear her name.

A tremor passed through him and when it had gone, it had taken the anger and need for revenge with it. His touch was gentle, but no less numbing. It was no longer a punishing force but a caress. When he opened his mouth over hers this time, enveloping it in devastating warmth, it was no longer the kiss of the conqueror, but of the conquered. He was no longer in control. Melissa had won, and the knowledge of it sent her soaring.

She squirmed under him, burrowing her face against the scratchiness of his chest. Now she was free to savor the heated scent of him and marvel at the texture of his skin and the thick hard muscles of his back beneath her fingers. What wonder there was in the delicate balance of strength and weakness that was Jeremy. What wonder there was in the power he had over her and in the power she had over him. The siege was over.

Tightening her arms around him, she pressed her soft lips against the side of his neck, wanting to claim a spot of her own.

His stomach muscles contracted and with a shuddering moan that might have been her own, he captured her lips again, again, and still again, until she thought she would self-destruct if he didn't make love to her.

"Is there anything about you that isn't perfect?" he said against her ear.

Odd. She had been thinking the same thing about him. About the utter and complete perfection of the man who held her heart as well as her body at his command.

"They knew exactly what they were doing when they chose you."

"They didn't choose me," she whispered almost fearfully, sensing a subtle change in him.

"Did you answer an advertisement in the newspaper?"

"Certainly not!"

"Wanted: one beautiful, desirable—perfect—woman. Must be completely irresistible."

The magic moment had flown. No, it hadn't flown. It had been driven back by Jeremy's iron will—a will that could only have been fed by hatred. Was it possible that he could hate her after what they had shared—or almost shared—a moment before?

She pressed her fingers against his lips. "Don't. Can't we forget what happened?"

"Forget? Years of torment? Do you have any idea of the hell my father went through? Of the guilt he carried to his grave?"

"I don't suppose it would be easy." The hollow ache began at the back of her throat again. If he needed to talk about it, she would let him. If she didn't, it would always wedge itself between them.

"How did they go about interviewing you?"

"They didn't. I wasn't hired." How many different ways would she have to say it? How many times?

"Did Hendricks try you out?"

This was too much. "Oh, Jeremy," she pleaded. "You mustn't."

"Or did he have to work with you awhile to break you in?"

She didn't answer immediately, thinking that sound of his question, hanging in the air, would make him realize the enormity of his insult. "Brian and I were only friends."

He turned away from her, to lie on his back and stare at the ceiling. "I suppose he never kissed you. Never made love to you. I suppose you never lay beside him as you're lying beside me now. You never told him you loved him."

"We never made love," she said fiercely.

"But you kissed him."

"Yes."

"And he stopped with that?"

"Yes."

"He doesn't look like that big a fool."

"I've told you. We were friends, nothing more."

"Do you think I've forgotten how he charged into the library that night, protecting his claim? Do you imagine I can forget how he looked when he saw you in my arms? It was the look of a jealous lover."

"He'd been drinking."

"What I saw wasn't drunkenness."

Her inner need to lash out was hammering at her now for allowing his brutal insinuations. How she contained her own anger and remained calm, she would never know. Except that perhaps the love she felt for Jeremy was that much stronger and worth the loss of her pride.

"How can I make you believe me?"

"Very easily. Tell me where to find you friend Hendricks."

"I don't know where he is."

"I'm supposed to swallow that?"

"It's true."

"Why shouldn't I believe it, huh?" He brought a hand to her throat, letting his thumb brush the vein. "I believed all the rest of it."

Unshed tears burned her eyes as he pulled himself away from her, stood up and reached for his shirt. "Where are you going?" she asked.

"I have to get out before I do something I'll regret." He stopped at the door but didn't look back. "I suggest you clear out as soon as possible. If you're still here when I come back, I might reconsider my position."

CHAPTER THIRTEEN

WHETHER OR NOT TO SAY her final goodbyes to Eli and his little people had been a momentous decision. Melissa had half promised to return one more time. Still, circumstances had changed. Supposing Jeremy came while she was there? She couldn't bear another scene. She didn't want to see him even if he behaved like a perfect gentleman for the older man's sake.

She pulled to the side of the road, debating heatedly with herself, and even drove partway out of town only to stop again and again before making a U-turn and coming back.

"It's the busiest time of the day for me and my friends," Eli said when he met her at the door, brushing aside her apologies for arriving so early. "Do you think any of these little hellions would allow me to sleep past six in the morning?"

He was right. The air was filled with a cacophony of squawks, cries and squeals that could have been interpreted as greetings, threats, warnings or simple expressions of joy. The shore was speckled with the white and gray of little feathered creatures inspecting the debris from yesterday's rain. Some of the birds were perched on rocks. Some were gliding. Others practiced their dives, and still others moved like arrows shot from bows.

"It's a beauty of a day, isn't it?" Eli remarked, squinting at the sky.

"Yes," Melissa agreed. "It's hard to believe there was a storm last night."

"The storm, yes. It took its toll." Eli invited her inside and, as he was busy with new arrivals, he set Melissa to mixing up a batch of egg custard for his invalids.

"I can't stay long," she told him.

He grunted. "Haven't worked things out with our boy yet?"

"They can't be worked out."

"So you scrap it all, the way you'd scrap a piece of knitting that turned out wrong?"

She swallowed hard, not wanting to discuss it, not even with Eli. She slid the pan off the burner, to scrape the bottom with a wooden spoon. "Sometimes that knitting is so twisted and tangled it's better to scrap it and start all over again."

"It's that easy, is it?" He hunched his shoulders and held up a flat palm. "Listen to me, jabbering like the busybodies I try to stay clear of."

"We're even, then," she admitted. "I'm guilty of forcing unwelcome advice on you, too."

But Eli's opening the door—mentioning Jeremy— had left her with an aching need to know more about the man she loved. The man she would now have to learn to stop loving.

But not yet.

She asked questions and Eli answered them. He told how their friendship had begun, with twelve-year-old Jeremy bringing him a pigeon he'd had to fight two bigger boys to rescue.

"Poor little tyke looked as much in need of doctoring as the bird," he said, chuckling at the memory.

"Oh, how he wept when that pigeon died. We buried her at the top of the hill in a metal cookie box. Her name was Valerie."

Eli talked about Kathryn too and how she and Jeremy had known each other for so long they were more like brother and sister than husband and wife.

"Frail as a little bird herself, she was. And pretty as one, too. Jeremiah tried to keep her alive through sheer willpower. When he couldn't, it was like he thought he'd failed her."

Maybe that feeling of failure to save a loved one had been the tie that bound him and Eli so closely, Melissa thought.

"Well now." Eli pushed back his chair with the resignation of someone who was about to do something he'd been putting off. "It's time to say goodbye to our friends."

"Are you sure?" Melissa asked. "It could rain again."

"Now you sound like me. Always inventing some excuse to keep them one more day." He swung the window down, allowing the chain to take its weight. It made a perfect platform for departing birds to use in their own time.

Illona hopped out first, gingerly pecking the air before going back again. For Murphy, however, there was no reluctant departure. He preened himself while his cage mate tested the takeoff point for him. Then he gave a little hop and soared out of sight.

So it hadn't worked out for them, either. Did birds feel rejected? Melissa wondered, thinking of poor Illona. Did they know heartbreak and loss?

Illona stood on one foot for a very long time, mulling over her decision. At last, she fluttered her wings, trying them, before gliding onto a nearby rock.

"Do you ever hope they won't go?" Melissa asked.

"Every single time. But they always do. Their world is out there. But let me tell you, once in a while, sometimes much later, one of them comes back." His lips trembled, and he pressed them together. "Ah, that's a feeling no man alive can know unless he's experienced it."

"I can imagine."

"Lookit there, will you, girl?" Eli's voice rose another octave as he pointed, stamping a foot on the ground.

Illona, who had hopped onto the sand to satisfy her curiosity about a bit of seaweed, had been joined by another bird of her kind. The bird, holding a small herring in its beak, dipped and bowed, seeming to offer the fish to her.

"He's back."

"But how can you know it's Murphy? So many of them look alike."

"It's him, sure enough. Watch. It's her turn now to be coy. They play the same games we humans play."

Illona hopped away and stood stretching her neck in apparent boredom. The other bird hopped after her, holding out its herring. He dropped it and strutted for a moment, then offered it again. With a quick pecking motion, she took it.

"Good for you, Murphy," Eli guffawed, digging an elbow into Melissa's side. "What did I tell you?"

"What does it mean?"

"Exactly what it means when a boy offers a girl a diamond ring."

"Oh, Eli," she scoffed. "It could mean she's hungry."

He narrowed his eyes. "And they say the male of the species is the cynic."

When Melissa looked back again, the two birds were flying away together. She clasped her hands and brought them to her mouth. Whether his interpretation of the scene was correct or not, she chose to believe it.

It was time. The sun was getting warmer, and she had a long way to go. Eli held out a hand, but she ignored it and kissed him on the cheek instead, hugging him close. "Goodbye. I'll never forget you."

"I don't expect you will. We'll meet again."

"It isn't likely."

His eyes twinkled all the more. "We'll see."

She was almost grateful for the long drive and the traffic that took too much of her attention to allow for thinking. Hoping to involve herself again with what was happening in the rest of the world, she tuned her radio dial to a news station and kept it there.

It struck her as the road signs announced that she was only seventeen miles from Albany. Much as she would have liked to go straight home, she couldn't. There was unfinished business, and if it wasn't too late, she had to tend to it.

She'd only been there once, on the day they'd begun their journey, when Brian had taken her to meet Natalie. But she found the elm-shaded street easily and the apartment house at the curve of the cul-de-sac.

Her brisk knocking didn't bring anyone at first. She was about to turn away when the door opened. Without waiting for Brian to invite her in, she thrust herself past him.

"Why?" she asked.

"Why?" He recovered quickly. "Money, kitten, money. Why does anyone do anything?"

She studied him, half-surprised to see the face still look so boyishly innocent. Something about his appearance should have changed to reflect the twisted moral character of the inner man. "All those lies!"

"Would you have cooperated if I'd told you the truth?"

"You know the answer to that."

"Well then?" He raked his fingers through his hair. "Hope you don't mind talking while I pack. If you found me here, it's a cinch York or the people at his beck and call will do the same. Natalie's already split."

Melissa followed him into the bedroom where dresser drawers were pulled open and two suitcases lay open. "I would have thought you'd have gone together."

"We had, shall we say, a falling out." He picked up a bottle of shaving lotion, held it up to the light to check how much was left and dropped it into a trash can. "Was there anything in particular you wanted?"

His matter-of-fact tone was almost laughable. Surprisingly cooperative, he answered her questions without hedging. Yes, Natalie had actually been pregnant with Jeremy's child when Harold York paid her to go away. He'd promised to take care of all expenses and to provide generous support payments until the child—boy or girl—turned eighteen. The only requirement was that she stay away and Jeremy never be told about it.

"The upstanding, self-righteous old bastard," Brian said through clenched teeth. "When Natalie miscarried in the third month, she didn't tell him. Let him go on paying as long as she could get by with it, she figured. Then she married Larry Kerr, a likable but penniless commercial artist. When they had a daughter, Nat juggled the dates and let the old man believe Jean was the child Jeremy had fathered. It wasn't hard. He didn't give a damn about details, and he sure wasn't going to carry any pictures of the little bundle of joy in his wallet."

"Wouldn't it have saved a lot of trouble if Natalie had convinced the real Jean to attend the bicentennial? I would think that on such an important occasion their differences could have been put aside."

"Attend it?" Brian pulled out one of the dresser drawers and emptied the contents on the bed. "We're lucky the kid didn't call York and blow the whistle on us. When she found out about the plot—eavesdropping, her greatest talent—you'd have thought we were planning to overthrow the government. She packed up and went to live with her father. Said she never wanted to see her mother again. It's good riddance, as far as I'm concerned."

"But Natalie wanted the money for Jean's musical education, didn't she?"

He stopped packing and smirked. "If you believe that, kitten, you'll believe anything. Jean plays very well and for a while had ambitions in that direction. But you know kids. Now she wants a career in outer space."

"You aren't really Natalie's brother, are you?"

"Hell, no," he snorted. "We met shortly after she and Larry called it quits. She noticed a surface resemblance that would let me pass as family, discovered that I was going through a few financial setbacks, shall we say, and offered me a good slice of the pie for posing as her brother. The real one is in California somewhere. It added a touch of authenticity to the tale, and as it turned out I was handy to keep you out of the way. That, by the way, I would have done for nothing.''

Melissa groaned and slapped away the hand that smoothed her cheek. ''And you don't feel guilty for the pain you've caused?''

''Do I cry over the Yorks? Hah! Why shouldn't they share some of the wealth? They've trampled on enough of us commoners to get where they are. Anyhow, thanks to that brainless little broad—'' He fluttered one hand. ''Sorry. Thanks to Arlene's getting dizzy over baby brother, Todd, we didn't get the pot of gold we'd expected to get.''

''At least I can be grateful for that.'' There was no point in going on with it, Melissa decided. Brian—or whoever he actually was—didn't even think he'd done anything wrong.

''Wait a second, kitten.'' He rushed ahead to bar the door. ''You're a bright kid. It probably isn't necessary to tell you this.''

''Well?''

''Your sister accepted payment in advance and by check for her role playing. If you decide to go to the authorities and turn us in, I'll see that she takes the fall, too.''

Melissa shook her head slowly. ''You played your part well,'' she said. ''You were terribly charming.''

''I'm a charming fellow,'' he agreed.

''And completely lacking in honor.''

''With honor and a couple of quarters, I can buy a cup of coffee,'' he sneered. ''Is there anything else I can do for you?''

''Nothing at all,'' she said, pushing past him.

CHAPTER FOURTEEN

ALBANY HAD BEEN SIZZLING when Melissa left, and it was sizzling when she returned.

Thanks to the careful attention of Marcia Hanning, who lived next door, the Creeping Charlie hadn't died of thirst and newspapers hadn't been allowed to accumulate on the lawn. The only sign of her absence was a stack of unopened letters waiting on the telephone stand, and perphaps the stuffy smell of an unaired house.

She had, herself, undergone so many changes, she'd half expected to feel as Rip Van Winkle had upon returning after his twenty-year snooze. The grass should have been waist high. The shrubbery should have been overgrown, and spider webs should have decorated the corners.

She moved around aimlessly, opening windows, unpacking and sorting mail. A week of her holiday remained, and as she figured it, there was a year of odd jobs to be finished. A rusting screen in Arlene's room needed replacing. A window over the kitchen sink was stuck from too many repaintings. The carpets needed shampooing. On and on. She'd made a list during her more ambitious, prevacation days. But she didn't know where she'd put it.

When the phone rang, she considered not answering. But then she had to. It could have been Arlene. It was.

"Oh, Sis. Am I glad I got you!" The girl sounded breezy and unperturbed by recent disaster. "I've been trying and trying."

"I haven't gone anywhere except to the market. Maybe I was in the yard."

Arlene and her new husband were still honeymooning in Connecticut about fifty miles from Sandgate. They'd been sailing every day and were having a wonderful time.

"Are you all right?" Arlene asked. "You sound funny."

"Vacation lag," Melissa said. "Have you seen Jeremy?"

"No. Todd called home and talked to him, though. Why?"

"No reason." She felt relieved, if a bit puzzled. Why hadn't Jeremy pounced on Arlene the way he'd pounced on her? "He can be difficult. I wouldn't let anything he says spoil things for you."

The younger girl wasn't listening. She was talking to someone in the background, probably Todd. "I have to run now," she said abruptly. "I'll be coming home on Friday in the late afternoon. Todd will be driving with me. I wonder—could you have the piano tuned?"

"I suppose so."

"And could you spruce things up some? Maybe cut some roses and put them in vases around."

"I'll do my best."

"One more thing. It would be fantastic if you could have dinner ready. Something that's good reheated, in case we're delayed. A pot of your scrumptious chili, maybe, and some French bread from the bakery to celebrate.''

"Why don't I hire a six-piece band?" Melissa asked the broken connection as her sister hung up without a proper goodbye.

Brushing off a feeling of melancholy, she went back to her bedroom and began to gather up the clothing that needed laundering. She had read somewhere that a person's experiences could be likened to pages in a gigantic notebook. Ruined ones could be ripped out and discarded and it would be as if they had never happened. Now the pages of her notebook that had to be tossed away and forgotten included Jeremy as well as Brian.

Where would she begin? Maybe if she offered a little encouragement to the new outside adjuster in auto claims, who'd been trying to get to know her for weeks, she'd discover they had something in common.

Then a fleeting memory of the man's Prince Valiant haircut and his snide wink when they met in the elevator made her groan inside. There had to be a less drastic way to keep busy.

The answer came as she drove past a paint and wallpaper store on her way home from the laundromat later. Arlene had asked if she could spruce things up a bit. So why didn't she?

The dining room was small and hopelessly dingy. There was no window and the cocoa brown her mother had chosen for the walls only made it appear smaller and dingier. Off-white, not only in the dining room, but in the living room as well, would push the walls back and give the entire house a more inviting look.

"Are you ever the ambitious one!" Marcia Hanning called as Melissa made trip after trip from car to house with paint, rollers and trays. "Did you buy one of those little sponge thingumajigs that makes it easy to do corners?"

"No. I figured to do the tricky parts with a brush."

"Surely you bought one of those long handles that screw into your roller. No? Oh, kid, take it from me. You'll need it to keep from getting a stiff neck." Marcia flung one sunburnt arm up to shield her eyes from the sun. "I have one. Somewhere."

"Don't bother about it," Melissa told her, backing toward the house. "I'm only doing two rooms."

"The last time we painted, my son cleaned the brushes. Maybe he knows where—"

"I don't need anything more. Really."

"All right." The woman shrugged one shoulder. "If I happen across those things though, I'll trot over with them. Don't forget—cold cream on your face and arms. Then if any paint drips on you, it'll wipe off easy."

After Melissa had pulled on the baggy jump suit she'd always used for messy jobs and stepped into a pair of out-at-the-toe sneakers, she covered her hair with a clean dust cloth and pinned it securely. Deciding that Marcia, who was an incurable do-it-yourselfer, knew what she was talking about, she dipped her fingers into a jar of cold cream and slathered it thickly on her face, neck and arms.

To begin with, all went well. The first few strokes previewed the fresher look that white would give the room. She hadn't taken into account, though, the rising heat of the day. The air was uncomfortably thick toward the ceiling, but laden with the smell of paint, it was almost overpowering.

As Marcia had predicted, her neck began to ache before she'd reached the halfway mark. Would it be worth cleaning up and getting dressed again to go back to the paint store to buy an extension handle?

As she considered the idea, she grew careless and a splotch of white hit her in the face. A dribble started down her arm and dropped onto her shoe. She sighed and rested for a moment, grateful at least for the cold cream that would make the cleanup easier.

"It's unlocked," she called when she heard the knock at the door. Thank goodness. It would be Marcia to the rescue with her painting equipment. She climbed down the ladder, laughing at the bedraggled spectacle she would present. "Come in."

"No! Don't come in," she cried, nearly kicking the paint can over when she saw Jeremy cross the threshold.

"Melissa?" he asked quizzically, as if he wasn't quite sure of her identity. He wore a pale yellow knit shirt that made his skin look bronzed, and his eyes very blue, rather than gray.

"Go away!" She waved him back. "How did you find me?"

"I had a check made of your license number."

"And my fingerprints? Were you surprised to find I didn't have a police record?"

He closed the door behind him and gingerly made his way toward her through the path left between drop cloths. "It'll take two coats," he said, studying the ceiling too intently.

"And what would you know about painting? You pick up a phone and order a batallion of painters to do the job for you." She was proud of the strength she had mustered in dealing with him and grateful for her numbed feelings. She'd already cried herself out. No more tears were left. She could look at him and feel only a hollow ache. Her inner defense mechanism was in perfect order.

"May I sit down?"

"May you sit down?" How ludicrous his politeness seemed after the savagery of their last meeting. "Not if you value your clothes." She indicated the spattered drop cloths with a careless gesture.

"In the kitchen then?"

"If you like." She pointed. "It's through that door."

"You know I meant both of us. I want to talk."

"I believe you can talk standing up. If I want to finish this afternoon—and I do—I'll have to keep at it."

He drummed his fingers against his side. "I didn't drive all the way from Sandgate for this."

"Why did you come?"

"For one thing, to return this to you." He offered a squarish box that looked as if it had once held jam. When she didn't take it from him, he opened it, reached inside and brought out a snowstorm paperweight. Flurries of white started up inside the glass. He watched her face intently for reaction. "You forgot it."

"I don't want it."

"Why not?"

She averted her eyes. "It would bring back too many ugly memories."

"And too many good ones?"

"Darned few!"

He reached out to her, but she stepped back quickly and held the dripping paint roller in front of her as if it were a spear. "Stay where you are, pal."

"You've got me covered." Jeremy laughed and raised his hands in token surrender. "If I were planning to take advantage of you, little one, that paint wouldn't stop me."

A vision of their last night together spun across the screen of her mind. The night he'd stripped her of her defenses and her pride. When she felt her cheeks coloring, she raised her chin and met his eyes in careful defiance. Predictably her heart began its syncopated beat. But she didn't waver.

"I keep forgetting," she said. "You aren't like the rest of the peasants. If your shirt gets ruined, you can ring up the store and order a dozen more to replace it. Can't you?"

His left eye narrowed, but if he was becoming angry, he managed to keep himself in check. He was a master of self-control by necessity. Who knows how many successful business deals had been made because of his uncanny knack to put on a winning, smiling front when he didn't mean it? "We both know I didn't drive here just to bring you this." He gave the globe a shake and set it on the mound that was the coffee table.

Melissa took a second look at it. Something had been added. A red-capped child stood beside the house inside the globe. "This isn't mine."

He grinned sheepishly. "I'd hoped you wouldn't notice. Yours is lost."

"How did it get lost?"

"It wasn't one of my better days and—I hurled it against the wall. Since it was my fault, I bought you another."

"I hope you don't expect me to thank you."

"I don't know what I expected." He slid a finger almost lovingly along the base of the paperweight and she was struck with a sudden suspicion.

"You didn't buy this for me."

"No. It belonged to my grandmother. I wanted you to have it."

"Then I can't take it. It belongs in your family."

He brought a hand to the back of his neck and rubbed. Was his neck bothering him again? Or was the gesture one of frustration? "Maybe you do, too."

She hardly heard him. "Maybe I—what?"

"Belong in my family."

"Have you forgotten?" she began, discarding his unlikely suggestion with a toss of her head. "My sister and I are conniving gold diggers, out for what we can get."

"A man in my position has to consider that."

"Oh." She twisted her face into an expression of exaggerated sympathy. "Poor little rich boy. So many women chasing you. And only for your money."

"You aren't going to let up, are you?"

"You can never be sure a woman loves you for yourself, can you?" she persisted. "Except that I don't buy it. Look at yourself, pal. You aren't exactly Frankenstein's monster. Not on the outside, anyway."

He grinned. "Thank you. I suppose that's the closest I'll ever get to a compliment from you."

"I suppose it is." Her heart was beating entirely too fast. She felt light-headed. The anger that had carried her this far was disintegrating. "Will you leave now and allow me to get back to my work?"

He turned away with a drawn-out sigh, but took only a single step. "It's been hell for me since you left, knowing I drove you away. I wanted to tell you that what's past is past. I'm willing to forget. None of it will ever be mentioned again."

Outside there was the clatter of metal wheels on the sidewalk. The children down the street were racing on their skateboards again. Melissa concentrated on the sound, counting on its familiarity to pull her to earth and to still the turmoil inside her.

She wasn't being hypnotized by Jeremy's eyes now. She wasn't being drugged by his lips or manipulated by the mastery of his touch. She was only looking at his back. His shoulders. The way his hair curled slightly at the nape of his neck. Yet she loved him so much, it was torment not to reach for him. Not to cry out that she would eagerly accept whatever terms he offered.

Until this moment she hadn't considered it possible to be furious with a man and still love that man so terribly at the same time. If Jeremy believed her guilty of treachery—and obviously he still did—their relationship could only be a shallow one. She'd rather not have him at all.

"That's mighty big of you, Mr. York," she added stiffly. "You're willing to forgive me."

"Melissa, I'm not very good at this."

"On the contrary, you're extremely good at it. Except that I didn't do anything to be forgiven for. You began, or rather, your father began paying Natalie when I was a child. Do you imagine I was an accomplice then?"

"I didn't say—"

"When I agreed to accompany the others to Sandgate, I knew nothing about the plot to make you believe Jean was your daughter. She isn't, by the way. Larry Kerr is her father."

"I know. I located him and saw the real Jean."

Determined to have it said, Melissa told her story from beginning to end. Once or twice he tried to interrupt, but she raised her voice to cover his.

"Are you finished?" he asked, when she'd run out of words.

"Completely."

He kicked at a corner of drop cloth as he turned back to face her. "I've been trying to tell you. Todd already gave me the facts. Arlene confessed to him and swore him to secrecy the night they met."

So much for Arlene's ability to keep a secret. Melissa should have known. "And so you believe me?" she asked.

A smile of relief curved on his lips. "Yes, with all my heart, I do."

"Because your brother told you." Her tone was accusing.

"What do you want me to say?" He slapped a hand to his forehead in frustration. "That I love you? You know damned well I do. Through all my worry about how I was going to handle my brother and the girl and even *if* I could handle what was happening between them, I found myself daydreaming about you incessantly. You've dug yourself so deep into my heart and mind I can't get free of you."

"But you've tried."

"Hell, yes. Why shouldn't I? You're the most—" He broke off all at once, realizing that he'd been shouting. "Okay." Painstakingly calm again, he held up both hands, palms toward her. "I want you to put away your paint things. Get changed and let me take you out to dinner. We've never really had any civilized time together. Only moments stolen here and there, colored by circumstances and hacked short by bickering. We've never talked. Really talked."

Melissa knelt to stir the paint again. How could she explain her feelings to him? How easily he spoke of love. Yet anger and impatience were ready to emerge at any moment. What if the part of him that claimed to want her now were to turn against her tomorrow? It would be shattering to get close to him and have him pull away again.

"I appreciate your offer," she said, "but as you can see, I'm in the middle of a task I have to finish. I want to get it over and done and the smell of paint gone by the time Arlene and Todd get home."

"You appreciate my offer?" he repeated dully. "You make it sound like a business deal gone sour. Didn't you hear a word I said?"

"I heard and I—"

"You appreciate it." He shook his head as if to clear it. "That's all you have to say?"

"What more is there?" She remained on her knees, staring into the paint can as though it were a magic cauldron and the act of stirring would make the pain of the moment vanish and Jeremy along with it.

"Nothing, I suppose. But you can't hang a man for trying." He stood quietly, wanting to give her a chance to change her mind. Then the roar of skateboards on the sidewalk exploded the excruciating stillness. He touched his forehead in a mock salute. "Goodbye, Melissa Brandon."

It sounded so final. It felt as though she were being ripped in two. Maybe she was wrong. Probably she was weak and foolish. But she couldn't allow him to walk out of her life. Finding a pearl in a lunch counter tuna fish salad would be more likely than finding another Jeremy.

"You haven't even suggested the obvious solution to the dilemma," she said. "If you were to help me, we could get the job done in half the time."

"You want to put me to work?" The half smile she'd once considered so maddeningly arrogant seemed anything but maddening now.

"Unless you don't think you can handle it."

He drummed an index finger against his chin in the manner of a corporate head pondering a weighty decision. "I can handle it. The question is, what do I get in return for my labor?"

Her heart began its crazed thudding again. "We'll talk about that later."

"You know a York doesn't do business that way." He came closer. "I want to talk about it now."

As she gazed up at him with moist eyes, she had to wage a terrific battle to keep from flinging herself into his arms. "There are some work clothes that belonged to my father on a hook just inside the utility closet on the service porch. They may be a bit—"

His lips descended on hers, silencing them, as he pulled her against him.

"You'll get paint on your clothes," she murmured against his mouth between ravenous kisses.

"Forget the work clothes," he said brokenly. "We won't need them."

"But your shirt and . . ."

"I won't wear the shirt either."

"But . . ."

A glint crept into his eyes. "The efficiency expert in me has a great idea. Why wear clothes at all?"

She laughed, imagining Marcia bursting in to find the two of them merrily painting in the altogether. "Silly!"

"Did I say something funny?" Jeremy tried to look innocent.

"No. Just impractical."

"What could be more practical? Think of the laundry we'd save."

"Think of the time we'd have, scrubbing up afterward," she countered.

"I am. That, lady, is where the fun comes in."

"Forget it, pal." She touched a clenched fist to his jaw in mock anger.

He kissed it. "Killjoy."

He tried for her lips again, and she drew back. "Jeremy, be careful. I have paint and—" His mouth took hers with growing hunger, and every muscle in her body seemed to go slack. "And cold cream all over my face," she finished weakly, allowing her eyes to close.

"That makes two of us."

Something told her that the painting had already progressed as far as it would that day. And maybe the next. With a sigh of supreme contentment, she slid her arms around his neck and if he hadn't lifted her off her feet and carried her, she would have floated skyward.

Six exciting series for you every month... from Harlequin

Harlequin Romance·
The series that started it all

Tender, captivating and heartwarming...
love stories that sweep you off to faraway places
and delight you with the magic of love.

◆

Harlequin Presents·
Powerful contemporary love stories...as individual as the women who read them

The No. 1 romance series...
exciting love stories for you, the woman of today...
a rare blend of passion and dramatic realism.

◆

Harlequin Superromance®
It's more than romance... it's Harlequin Superromance

A sophisticated, contemporary romance-fiction
series, providing you with a longer,
more involving read...a richer mix of complex plots,
realism and adventure.

Harlequin
American Romance™
Harlequin celebrates the American woman...

...by offering you romance stories written about American women, by American women for American women. This series offers you contemporary romances uniquely North American in flavor and appeal.

◆

Harlequin Temptation
Passionate stories for today's woman

An exciting series of sensual, mature stories of love...dilemmas, choices, resolutions... all contemporary issues dealt with in a true-to-life fashion by some of your favorite authors.

◆

Harlequin Intrigue
Because romance can be quite an adventure

Harlequin Intrigue, an innovative series that blends the romance you expect... with the unexpected. Each story has an added element of intrigue that provides a new twist to the Harlequin tradition of romance excellence.

Harlequin Books

PROD-A-2